AN UNLIKELY
SPY

This book is dedicated to the members of the SOE, heroes far braver than any in stories.

AN UNLIKELY SPY

SPY

TERRY DEARY

BLOOMSBURY EDUCATION
LONDON   OXFORD   NEW YORK   NEW DELHI   SYDNEY

BLOOMSBURY EDUCATION
Bloomsbury Publishing Plc
50 Bedford Square, London, WC1B 3DP, UK

BLOOMSBURY, BLOOMSBURY EDUCATION and the Diana logo are trademarks of
Bloomsbury Publishing Plc

First published in Great Britain in 2019 by Bloomsbury Publishing Plc
Text copyright © Terry Deary, 2019

A catalogue record for this book is available from the British Library

ISBN: PB: 978-1-4729-6270-6; ePDF: 978-1-4729-6271-3; ePub: 978-1-4729-6269-0

2 4 6 8 10 9 7 5 3 1

Typeset by Newgen KnowledgeWorks Pvt. Ltd., Chennai, India
Printed and bound in CPI Group (UK) Ltd, Croydon, CR0 4YY

To find out more about our authors and books visit www.bloomsbury.com
and sign up for our newsletters

'I must go and meet with danger there,
Or it will seek me in another place.'

William Shakespeare – *Henry IV, Part 2*

Part I

Chapter One

'He saved the lives of the men who killed my brother'

Sunday, 3 September 1939: Castle Bromwich, England

Brigit Furst was not a popular girl. The girls in her class tried to bully her. Brigit Furst didn't care.

'You talk funny,' Gladys Turnbull would sneer. And it was true. Brigit didn't talk with the same English Midlands accent as the other girls.

Brigit wasn't all that pretty, so Gladys and her gang couldn't envy her good looks, but she did have glossy red-brown hair that shone in the September sun. Like the others in the class, her school uniform was frayed and worn, but always clean as rainwater.

'Clean as the queen,' the gang sneered. Yet they didn't really hate her for that.

No. Brigit's real crime, in the mean little eyes of Gladys, was being too *clever*. Tests? Brigit always came top of the class. Exams to get to grammar school? Brigit would sail through and Gladys would fail, they all knew that.

'Miss Smarty Pants,' Gladys jeered, so jealous she made her thin pale face turn red with rage. 'Let's get her.'

Not everyone hated Brigit. Jessie Burdess wondered at Brigit's brains and trembled at Gladys's spite. She met Brigit at the school gate that September morning. Jessie's eyes were wide and her breath came in gasps. 'Brigit, oh Brigit,' she panted. 'You'll never guess what Gladys Turnbull's done now.'

Brigit stopped and looked at her fair-haired friend. 'No, Jessie, I'm sure I won't. Far better if you just tell me.'

Jessie's words tumbled out. 'She's got a pepper pot in her school bag and she's going to wait till you leave your gas mask in your desk at break time, and then she's going to put pepper in the mask so when we do gas-mask practice with Miss Dennison it's going to blind you and choke you and make you sneeze as soon as you try to breathe.'

Brigit patted the dull cardboard gas-mask box that hung round her neck on a string. She sighed. 'Thank you, Jess. Forewarned is forearmed,' she said as she marched towards the classroom door.

'What does that mean?'

Brigit gave a small smile. 'It means that now you've told me, I can plan what I'm going to do about it.'

The class were shouting and arguing, gossiping and gabbling, as Brigit and Jessie walked in. The noise dropped a little. Brigit calmly and carefully placed her gas-mask box on her desk, then turned her back on it.

Brigit walked to the blackboard and picked up the rubber. She began to clean off the chalk. By now the class was almost silent so the girl could hear the soft scuff as someone lifted the cardboard lid. Someone giggled, then the lid was closed again.

Brigit turned in time to see Gladys Turnbull slip a wooden pepper pot into her school satchel. Gladys looked guilty. 'Cleaning the blackboard won't make Miss Dennison like you,' she snarled.

Brigit gave her warmest smile. 'I know.'

For once the mask of hate slipped from Gladys's thin face. 'You're the cleverest girl in the class... except me, of course. But Miss Dennison hates you. Why's that?'

'Her brother died in the Great War,' Brigit said. 'So?'

Before Brigit could answer, the door was thrown open and banged against the doorstop. Miss Dennison's face was wrinkled like an old cooking apple and twice as bitter. There was a scrambling and scraping as the girls threw themselves on to the wooden benches behind their desks. 'Why are you out of your seat, Brigit Furst?' the teacher asked sourly.

'I was cleaning the blackboard for you, Miss Dennison. So it would save you the trouble and give you more time to share your wisdom with us.'

Miss Dennison's eyes went narrow as she looked to see if Brigit's words were meant as insolence. She placed her gas-mask box on her high desk. 'If I want my blackboard cleaned then I'll ask someone I can trust, not some grubby little kraut,' she snapped.

'What's a kraut, miss?' Jessie Burdess asked.

'Never mind,' the teacher muttered. 'You have been called into school today, a Sunday, for an important announcement. But you will treat it like any other school day. This morning's assembly will take place at eleven o'clock.'

'Why, miss?' Jessie asked.

The teacher glared and spoke slowly. 'Because Mr Cutter has said so. And it is not our business to question the headmaster's orders.' Then her words came out machine-gun fast. 'What is it not our business to do, Jessie Burdess?'

Frightened, Jessie swallowed hard and whispered, 'It is not our business to order Mr Question's cutter.'

The teacher shook her head. 'We will study history for ninety minutes, have our morning break, and then go straight to the hall. Susan Wilson, help me give out the history books.'

Miss Dennison opened the door to a book cupboard in the wall, turned on the light and disappeared inside, followed by the smallest girl in the class. Brigit rose to her feet, took her gas mask carefully from its box and walked silently to the teacher's desk. She opened Miss Dennison's gas-mask case, took out the glass, rubber and metal mask inside, and replaced it with her own. She put Miss Dennison's mask in her own box and sat down, folding her hands on the scarred desktop.

The class gasped, then fifty children seemed to hold their breaths as the teacher came out of the cupboard and ordered Susan Wilson to give out the dusty books.

Gladys Turnbull's face lit up and she raised a hand. 'Please, miss.'

'Yes, what is it, girl?'

Brigit turned and looked across at her enemy two seats away. She pointed at Gladys's satchel and mouthed the words, 'Who has the pepper pot in her bag?'

Gladys's mouth went dry as she muttered, 'I like history, miss. Can we do the bit where Dick Turpin rode Black Beauty from London to York?'

The teacher tried not to look pleased. 'It was Black *Bess*, Gladys, not Black Beauty. But I like that story too. Open your books at page one hundred and ninety-seven and let us take turns at reading around the class. Begin, Gladys.'

A fly buzzed against the grimy window and the droning noise was as dull as the reading. The pupils wrote a story in their dark red (history) exercise books: 'My great race, by Black Bess'.

At last Miss Dennison passed a handbell to a girl by the door and told her to ring it in the corridor to signal break. 'Leave your gas masks on your desks and go out to play,' the teacher ordered.

Brigit fussed with her pencil case, so she was the last one left in the room and her gas mask was guarded. 'Out, kraut,' Miss Dennison snarled.

Brigit closed her eyes for a moment then looked at her teacher. 'My father is German. I was born in France. We moved here to escape the hatred of the French. We thought the British would be more forgiving.'

The teacher put her podgy hands on the girl's desk and leaned forward so she was breathing in her face. She smelled like an ashtray. 'I will be forgiving when you bring my brother back to life. Your father was one of the Huns that killed him.'

'My father acted as a nurse in the Great War. He killed nobody.'

Miss Dennison smiled, showing her light brown teeth. 'He saved the lives of the men who killed my brother. It's the same thing. I am ashamed to have a German in my class, and I will be glad when you leave.'

'I am French,' Brigit said calmly. 'But I shall be so sorry to leave the best teacher I've ever had.' She gave a little sniff of sorrow. 'Probably the best teacher in the whole of Castle Bromwich.'

Miss Dennison's mouth opened but she couldn't find any words. 'Out,' she finally croaked.

Brigit turned away with a secret smile and left.

Chapter Two

'Today we are expecting an important announcement'

The children shuffled their feet on the floor of the school hall; there were sniffs and coughs, but no one spoke. Two hundred pairs of eyes turned to the door in the corner. Mr Cutter, the head teacher, marched in with a cane under his arm. His black hair was shiny as wet coal, held down with a greasy hair cream. His one eye glared at the children, but his glass eye scared them more.

'His eye was poked out with a German bayonet in 1917,' Jessie Burdess squeaked one day.

Billy Anderson snorted. 'I heard he got drunk and fell off his bike in 1933.'

Mr Cutter spoke and the pupils held their breath. Billy Anderson sneezed. 'Today we are expecting an important announcement. It will be on the radio and everyone in Britain will be listening, I am sure. Be silent or take a thrashing from my cane like you have never been thrashed before... not even you, Billy Anderson.'

Billy had badly cut hair that bristled like a wet cat's fur and his wide blue eyes were horrified. 'I never did nothing.'

Mr Cutter lunged forward, brought the cane down with a swoosh and held it under Billy's nose. 'I never did anything,' he hissed.

'I never said you did,' Billy gasped.

'Not me. You. You should say "I did nothing", or "I never did anything". But to say I never did nothing is a double negative and means you did something. Do I make myself clear?'

Billy shook his head. 'If *you* never did nothing and *I* never did nothing, then who did it?' he asked.

'Shut up, idiot,' the teacher roared. 'I'll deal with you later.' He turned on his heel and switched on the radio that stood on the platform. After a minute the valves grew warm with the smell of burning dust and the speaker hissed. At last a voice grew louder and clearer.

'This morning the British Ambassador in Berlin handed the German government a final note stating that, unless we heard from them by eleven o'clock that they were prepared at once to withdraw their troops from Poland, a state of war would exist between us. I have to tell you now that no such undertaking has been received, and that consequently this country is at war with Germany.'

He went on to talk about Britain and France going to help Poland. But Brigit's father and mother had already told her that would never happen. France would be invaded before the French armies could move. Britain would be alone.

And her father would be one of the enemy.

Mr Cutter paced across the stage in the school hall, waving his cane. 'We are at war. The soldiers, sailors and airmen will do the fighting. But those of us who are not fighting must do all we can to support them.' He raised his chin and looked at some distant point far outside the window. 'We must all do our bit.' There was a long silence. 'What must we do, Jessie Burdess?'

'Our bit, sir,' Jessie said, in awe at the very thought.

'What bit is that then?' Billy Anderson said. He had stuck his hand in the air but hadn't waited to be asked to speak.

Mr Cutter lowered his gaze to the boy. 'Good question, Billy Anderson. Good question.'

Billy almost blushed under the grime on his face.

The teacher began to pace again. 'Soon there will be less food to go around. Mr Hitler's submarines will patrol the seas and try to sink our food ships, so we starve to death. Every potato and carrot you can grow will help to defeat his wicked plan.'

'So growing a carrot is doing a bit... and growing two carrots is two bits?' said Billy.

'It is, Billy Anderson. But it's not just about carrots. It's about facing danger and showing no fear. Every time you face danger with courage, you are doing your bit.'

'But we're not in any danger here,' Gladys Turnbull argued. 'Not like the soldiers.'

Mr Cutter looked at the young eyes staring up at him. He cleared his throat and spoke carefully. 'Do not panic. I do not want anyone to panic. Understand? But very soon Mr Hitler will be dropping bombs on Britain.'

So the children panicked and whimpered and looked to the ceiling. 'I said I do not want you to panic,' the head screamed as the sounds of fear faded. 'The evil *German* dictator – yes *German* like Brigit Furst – will send his bombers. But our Spitfire planes will blow them out of the sky before they get as far as Castle Bromwich. And all the while the Spitfire factory in our town will be making hundreds of new planes to shoot down the thousands of bombers Germany will send. And Germany will send more planes to bomb our factories. Who can blame them?'

The children shuffled uneasily and looked out of the high hall windows for black-winged bombers. 'What if they miss the factories, sir? They could hit our house,' Gladys Turnbull cried.

'Good point, Gladys, but you do not have to worry about a bomb missing the factory and landing on your head. Why not, anyone?' he asked.

'Please, sir, because we're going to be excavated,' Jessie Burdess said in a quavering voice. Tears burst from her pale eyes. 'I don't want to go,' she moaned. Other boys and girls joined in the sobbing.

Mr Cutter swished at the air. 'Fine. Fine. Stay here and have a German bomb land on your head. You'll not be crying then. You'll be running to the railway station to get yourselves excavated... I mean *evacuated*.'

'Please, sir,' Brigit asked. 'How can we run for the railway station if a German bomb lands on our head?'

Mr Cutter's lips pulled back in a fierce sneer. 'I might have expected a wisecrack from a German brat like you. I dare say you'll be one of the ones putting a light on your roof to guide the enemy bombers to strike. Won't you?'

Brigit smiled and shook her head slowly. 'Why would I want to guide a German bomber to drop a bomb on me? I'd be better putting a light on the roof of *your* house, so they could blow up a British hero like you... sir.'

'Don't you dare,' the teacher shouted and his glass eye almost popped out. He took a deep breath. 'Anyway, you don't know where I live,' he finished savagely.

Brigit just gave a wise smile as if to say, 'Are you sure about that?'

'Now, your evacuation plans are in a letter you must take home. But before you leave, Miss Dennison here will take you through a gas-mask drill. I hope you've all remembered your gas masks?'

'I left mine on the tram,' Billy Anderson moaned.

'Then you can choke to death while the rest of us walk the streets gas-free and fearless,' Mr Cutter said. 'When Mr Hitler's bombers attacked Poland, they attacked hard and fast before the Poles could defend themselves. Bombs rained down from the skies as tanks drove in over the land.'

'Didn't the bombs fall on the tanks then?'

'Shut up, Billy Anderson. Now, this sort of attack is called a Lightning War – a *Blitzkrieg* in German. So there is your new word for today. *Blitzkrieg* – or Blitz,' he went on, chalking the word on a blackboard by the side of the stage. 'Everyone say it after me... Blitz.'

'Blitz.'

'A lightning attack, and there may be gas bombs mixed in with the explosive ones. So always carry your gas mask. Another example of how we can each do our bit. If you don't, then the wardens may arrest you. What must you always carry with you, Billy Anderson?'

'A handkerchief, my mum says, so I don't have to wipe my nose on my sleeve.'

Mr Cutter's good eye looked up at the ceiling in despair. 'Carry on, Miss Dennison. Show them how to put on their gas masks.'

Chapter Three

'A German has booby-trapped my mask'

The Class 4 teacher waddled on to the stage and used a ruler to point to a poster pinned up on the wall. The pupils had seen it all over the city and knew the words on it by heart, but the teacher read them out anyway. She took her own gas mask out of its case and showed the pupils what to do.

'*Firstly, you must hold your breath.*' Her cheeks turned into red balloons, but she had to let out her breath to give the next part of the instructions.

'*Hold the mask in front of your face with your thumbs inside the straps... like this.*'

Gladys Turnbull's mouth fell open and her gaze fell on the pepper pot poking out of her school bag.

'*Thrust the chin well forward into the mask... like this... and...*'

There was silence. Then a scream muffled by the rubber mask. Miss Dennison ripped the mask off her face and choked and spat and sneezed and rubbed at her red-raw eyes. 'Gassed,' she managed to hiss. 'I've been gassed. I'm blind. Oh, help, Mr Cutter. A German has booby-trapped my mask,' she sobbed.

Mr Cutter put an arm round the teacher's shoulders and led her away to the staffroom. Mr English, the seniors' teacher, stepped forward. 'Put your gas masks away and listen carefully. After assembly, you will all be going home. As you leave, the school secretary will hand you a letter. It is a letter for your parents. It will instruct them on Operation Pied Piper. Now, who knows the story of the Pied Piper?'

A pigtailed girl from Class 3 shot her hand into the air. 'Please, sir, it was a story about a wicked piper who got rid of all the rats in the city. But the city refused to pay him, so he came back and took all the children into the mountains.' Her face twisted into one of horror. 'And he shut them in a cave and they suffocated and died and nobody ever saw them alive again. Or even dead.'

Mr English looked as though he wished he hadn't asked. 'The Pied Piper led all the children to a *safe* place in the country. And our Operation Pied Piper will lead all of you to a safe place. A lovely new home in the country, far from the bombs.'

The children believed the girl from Class 3. They didn't believe the teacher. 'Go straight home to pack,' he snapped. 'School is now closed. Tomorrow you will be evacuated. Don't forget your letters. And don't open them before you get home. Or Mr Cutter will cane you.'

'Please, sir, how can he cane us if we're excavated to the country?' Jessie Burdess asked.

'Maybe he has a very long cane,' Billy Anderson sniggered.

Mr English glared at the boy. 'Many of the teachers will travel with you and some will stay to teach you in your new schools.'

A groan ran around the hall. 'I thought we were going to escape,' Gladys Turnbull muttered. 'It'll be as bad as this dump, but with sheep and cows.'

'Stand,' Mr English ordered. The pupils climbed stiffly to their feet and shuffled into lines.

Gladys slipped the pepper pot into Billy Anderson's jacket pocket as they joined the queue to leave the school hall. She glared at Brigit Furst. 'Poor Miss Dennison was right. It *was* a German that poisoned her mask. And we're going to get our revenge for that, aren't we, Jessie?'

Jessie blinked like a mole in sunlight. 'Not me. I'm going to be excavated.'

Brigit walked behind Gladys and Jessie. 'I'm going to open the letter. See what it says.'

'You can't do that,' Jessie gasped.

'Jess, this is about what's going to happen to us,' said Brigit. 'We need to know.'

Gladys glared at her but Brigit smiled, tore open the flap on her letter and handed it to Jessie to read. 'There's the train times for tomorrow, then there's two lists of clothes... vests and knickers, socks, blouse and cardigan. It says they're the things you must send with your evacuee. Then there's *another* list of things you might *like* to pack in your child's suitcase – overcoat and wellies, comb and toothbrush, boots and gym shoes... and packets of food.'

'Pah,' Gladys snorted. 'Why don't they just have one list?'

'Because not everyone in our class has wellies and an overcoat, boots and a toothbrush.' Brigit spoke quietly. 'Billy Anderson hasn't.'

'Why not?' Jessie asked and swallowed tears.

'His mother can't afford much,' Brigit explained.

Gladys turned on her furiously. 'That's right. Billy's dad was gassed in the last war. It took him a dozen years to die but the gas finally did for him soon after Billy was born. The gas *your* dad poisoned him with,' she raged at Brigit, delighted to have something new to goad her with. She tugged at Jessie's sleeve. 'Come on, Jess. I told you we're going to get her, and we are.'

Jessie Burdess was dragged down the road and into the black-brick rows of crumbling old houses. Half the gas lamps had been broken but no one walked those streets after dark anyway.

Brigit frowned. She wondered what Gladys's plot was. It didn't take her long to find out.

Chapter Four

'It's full of sheep isn't it?'

The milkman, Adam Bell, had finished his morning round and his horse was plodding over the cobbled street, the milk bottles rattling in their crates. 'Good day, Mr Bell,' Brigit called, but the sour-faced old man just glared at her, spat into the gutter, then rattled the reins to make the old horse hurry past. Brigit shrugged. Someone else who hated her for being half-German.

She let herself into her home, expecting it to be empty, and was surprised to hear a radio blaring out news of the war and the dangers the country faced. 'Maman?' she called.

'In the kitchen,' Aimee Furst called back. Brigit hung her school coat on the stand in the hall and looked back at the front door. It was solid oak and painted blue. It would have made the hallway dark but above the door was a window that let in some light. The window was of stained-glass panels that made a picture of a sunrise over gentle green and very English hills. The scarlet and lemon of the sun's rays in the pale blue skies over emerald fields always made Brigit feel warm and safe.

She hurried towards the kitchen where a second surprise was waiting for her. Her father, Marius, sat there with a cup of tea in front of him.

'Dad? Why aren't you at the factory?' she asked.

Marius shrugged. 'They sent me home,' he said slowly, staring into his saucer. 'Castle Bromwich will start to make Spitfire aeroplanes soon. It will be a top-secret place. They don't want a German working there... not even as a doctor doing their first aid.'

'Tea?' Aimee asked her daughter and started pouring a cup before Brigit could nod. 'Sorry, no milk,' she said. 'Mr Bell must have forgotten us.'

Brigit nodded, but even her fierce spirit was suddenly slipping under the tide of hatred that was washing around the family.

'I suppose your school sent you home too, Maman? The same as us?'

Aimee Furst was a teacher. 'Yes, the children were sent home to prepare for evacuation. You all leave tomorrow morning.'

'Me too?' Brigit said, pretending to be surprised. 'But I'll be as safe here as anywhere in the country if the Ger— if the enemy starts to bomb us.'

'No,' Marius said quietly. 'The Spitfire factory will be a target. When the bombers miss the factory, they could hit anywhere in our town. They won't be aiming for some village in Wales.'

'Wales? Is that where you want me to go?' Brigit said. 'It's full of sheep isn't it?'

Aimee nodded. 'The enemy won't waste bombs on farms. Even in the last war my parents' farm in France, in the middle of the war zone, was spared because both sides needed the food we produced.'

Brigit opened her mouth to argue but was stopped. What happened next was so swift and unexpected she remembered it for the rest of her life. First came the faint sounds of children in the street, stamping and jeering.

Then a sudden silence.

The family rose from the table to find out what was happening.

Before they reached the kitchen door they heard the sound of shattering glass and a heavy thump on the rug in the hall.

Brigit was first to the door and pulled it open. September air blew through the place where the window over the front door had been. The stained glass lay on the rug like spilled jewels from a treasure chest… amethyst and ruby, emerald and amber. In the middle of the glittering ruins of the window sat an ugly half-brick. Wrapped around it was a piece of paper tied with brown string.

Marius Furst strode past his daughter, crunched over the broken glass and pulled open the front door. When Brigit joined him, she looked out to see a dozen children in school uniform racing round the corner of their street. Only one boy

27

stood there, rooted as a hedge, with his mouth hanging open.

'Did you do this?' Marius asked.

The boy nodded dumbly.

'Billy,' Brigit said to her classmate. 'Why?'

He licked his pale lips and found his voice. 'Because Gladys Turnbull told me to,' he croaked.

Marius glared at him. 'Stay there. I am calling the police.'

But Billy found his legs as well as his tongue and turned to race after the others. Marius walked to the telephone on the hall table and dialled zero. 'Hello? Operator? Can you put me through to the Castle Bromwich police house, please? Yes… it is urgent.'

While he waited, Aimee picked up the brick and unfastened the string. She opened the paper. 'Jerman natzis,' Brigit read. 'Terrible spelling. Must be Gladys.'

'Hello? Police?' her father was saying. 'A mob of kids has just thrown a brick through the window above our door. Yes, we know who it was… at least my daughter knows them from school. My name? Marius Furst,' he went on, and gave the address.

He turned to his wife and daughter and said, 'They are sending a constable.'

Her father hadn't closed the front door, so Brigit was able to see when a black Wolseley Wasp pulled up outside. The sign above the car's windscreen said 'Police'. Two men in navy suits and black homburg hats stepped out and came through the front gate.

'They don't look like constables to me,' said Brigit.

'They were amazingly fast,' Aimee said, nervous and uncertain. 'Are you from Castle Bromwich police house?' she asked the men.

The older man, who was so broad the buttons on his waistcoat seemed as if they would burst, looked past her to her husband. 'Mr Furst?' he asked. 'Mr Marius Furst?'

'I am Doctor Furst,' Marius said, walking carefully over the broken glass towards the door. 'Who are you?'

'Detective Sergeant Fitzgerald,' the man said. 'I have some important business to carry out, and then my friend here can tell you what he wants.'

The sergeant reached into his pocket, took out a pair of handcuffs, and pulled Marius towards him to fasten them on his wrists. He spoke in a husky voice as if he were reading from a rulebook. 'Mr Furst... I am arresting you.'

Chapter Five

'Don't go hiding no guns or bombs in there'

Marius stood calmly and raised his chin a little. 'It is *Doctor* Furst, if you please.'

'*Mister* Furst, you have been identified as an alien. It is my duty to take you into custody for relocation to an internment camp for the duration of the war.'

'Marius hates the Nazis. That's why he left Germany years ago,' Aimee objected fiercely. 'He's a doctor in the Castle Bromwich aeroplane factory. He's helped dozens of workers setting up the Spitfire production line. It's your friends who will suffer if you lock him away.'

The policeman sniffed. 'Working in the Castle Bromwich aeroplane factory will give him the perfect chance to spy on the work that's going on there. He can report back to his mates in Germany and guide them to the factory.'

'That's stupid,' Aimee exploded.

'Stupid, am I?' The sergeant's eyes went narrow. 'Mrs Furst… you are *French*, aren't you?' Before she could answer he went on in a low voice. 'It's just as well the French are on our side or we'd have you in the internment camp with *Mister* Furst here. I'll wait while you pack him a case. But I warn you, the case will be searched before it is handed to him so don't go hiding no guns or bombs in there. Just spare clothes and a toothbrush. Oh, and don't forget the gas mask. It will be such a shame if his German friends drop gas bombs and traitors like *Mister* Furst choke to death.'

Aimee turned on her heel and hurried inside the house. 'How long will you keep him?' Brigit asked.

'Weren't you listening?' the policeman barked. 'For. The. Duration. Of. The. War. Do you know what that means, little girl?'

Brigit shrugged. 'Yes, I *do* know what it means. Would you like me to explain it to you? It means: For. As. Long. As. The. War. Lasts.'

The sergeant's eyes bulged as dangerously as his waistcoat buttons. 'You're half-German, *little* girl. If I had my way we'd be locking you up with your father.'

Brigit clapped her hands in front of her nose in a mock-childish glee. 'Ooooh, would you, *big* man? I'd like that.'

The sergeant took a deep breath. He looked at the front door and gave a thin smile. 'I see someone has already told you what they think of your type.'

'The constable is on his way,' Brigit said.

'No, he isn't. A war started today. The police have hundreds of important things to do – arresting spies like this for a start.'

Detective Sergeant Fitzgerald gave a savage tug on her father's handcuffs and led him to the car. He opened the back door and bundled Marius roughly inside. He turned back to Brigit. 'No one is going to investigate a broken window, little girl. No one.'

'A bit like Mr Hitler's Germany, then,' Brigit said with a loud sigh. 'The Germans turned on the Jews and smashed all their shop windows. They called it *Kristallnacht* – the Night of Broken Glass.'

'So?' the policeman hissed.

'So, the Nazi police stood by and watched the windows being smashed and didn't lift a finger to help. If we are at war with Mr Hitler's Nazis, why are you behaving like one? Will you be happy if they win and march into Britain? I'm sure they'll love to find people like you in the police.'

Detective Sergeant Fitzgerald raised a huge hand to slap Brigit, but the younger man stepped forward and grabbed the sergeant's wrist. The policeman breathed heavily for a few moments then shook off the hand that held his wrist. A look of fear, or respect, crossed his wide face. He lowered his hand and then his head. He glared angrily at the path.

At that moment Aimee appeared on the doorstep with a small brown cardboard suitcase and a gas-mask box. 'Don't I get to say goodbye to my husband?' she asked.

The sergeant snarled. 'They may let you visit him if you're lucky.'

'Not if you send him to a camp in Scotland or somewhere hundreds of miles away.'

The sergeant spread his hands. 'In this case you're in luck, my Frog friend. The camp has been set up on the golf course.'

'Which golf course?' Brigit asked.

The sergeant gave a brown-toothed grin. 'Hodgehill. A mile down the road.' He leaned towards Brigit and whispered, 'Your mum will be able to visit you both when I get a warrant to lock you away with your dad, eh?'

The other man had patiently stood silent while all this was going on. He didn't move towards the car when Detective Sergeant Fitzgerald climbed into the driver's seat and started the engine.

Brigit looked at her stony-faced mother. 'What shall we do, Maman?'

'We can start by sweeping up the glass and filling the gap with cardboard to keep the draught out.' She turned and began to walk back inside.

'Mrs Furst?' The younger man spoke for the first time. 'Aimee?' He raised his hat to show a kindly face and dark hair that was starting to go grey at the sides. 'You don't remember me, do you?'

Aimee Furst's eyes widened. She swayed as if her knees were going to give way and clutched at the frame of the door.

'It can't be,' she murmured, and tears sprang to her eyes.

Chapter Six

'You know Mr Churchill?'

'Come in, Captain Ellis,' Aimee Furst said. The man smiled at Brigit and followed them into the house.

He frowned when he saw the broken glass in the hallway. 'Can I help you clear this up?' he offered.

Aimee shook her head. 'Don't worry about that now,' she said as she pointed to a chair at the kitchen table. 'Can I make you some tea, Captain?'

'Yes please… and it's Major Ellis now.'

Aimee smiled. 'I thought you would be a general at least.'

The man laughed. 'In the secret service we don't go around flashing gold buttons and badges.'

'You wouldn't be secret then, would you?' Brigit said.

'Good afternoon,' Major Ellis said, turning to her. 'You must be Brigit. I've heard a lot about you. Your mother was a wildcat when she was your age. I've learned from your school you're just as bad.'

'Just as *good*,' Brigit corrected him. 'But how do you know what my mother was like at my age? That must have been during the last war.'

'It was,' Aimee said. 'I was a schoolgirl in Bray-on-Somme in France. The British had a spy in their army and I helped prove he was a traitor.'

Brigit's eyes sparkled. 'Was that when you helped Dad get back to Germany? You told me about that. But not the bit about the spy.'

Aimee nodded silently.

Major Ellis tapped the table with his finger. 'She helped your father escape at the same time as they were *both* being chased by Silver Hand and his partner.'

'Silver Hand?' Brigit asked.

'We called him that because he had a false metal hand,' the major explained. 'Your mother risked her life several times, helped the British army to win the war *and* saved your father from a prison camp or worse.'

'You didn't tell me you helped the British win the war, Maman,' Brigit said, cross and accusing.

Aimee Furst closed her eyes. 'I was machine-gunned by a German aeroplane, your father and I were trapped in a church tower and chased by a tank. I was pursued for miles by German soldiers and saw my lovely town in smoking ruins. I passed through stinking trenches and wasted woodlands.'

'So brave and so young,' Major Ellis muttered but Aimee's mind was still in the world of over twenty years ago.

'We were hiding down a well when the spies found us and pointed a gun to our heads. It took a brave old Frenchman to save us in the end. They were days of horror and hunger, terror and terrible sights. We saw so much death and we were close to death so many times – times when we were quite sure we were going to die.'

'Dad saved you?' Brigit asked.

Aimee nodded but Major Ellis cut in. 'It wasn't that simple. Your maman saved Marius just as many times as he saved her. And he was an enemy. She could have left him to die, but she didn't. Saving your enemy takes a far greater person than the one who simply saves a friend.'

Aimee shook her head to clear it of the memories. 'I still have nightmares about it. Twenty years ago, and I'm still haunted by the man with the silver hand. I didn't want to share those dreadful days with you, my love.'

Brigit nodded. 'But you were a hero. You and Dad. You should have got a medal.'

Aimee shrugged. 'It wasn't that important. We all did what we could to help France win the war. Your grand-maman Colette was as brave as me. She was part of a group called the White Lady that carried secret messages to the British about the German army. If she'd been caught, they'd have shot her. We all did what we could,' she said, avoiding her daughter's stern gaze.* Major Ellis smiled gently.

* You can read about Aimee's adventures in the First World War in *The Silver Hand*.

'So, Major, why are you here?' Aimee asked.

'Because we need your help… again.'

'Help? Help Britain?' Brigit said, angry now. 'When you've just taken Dad away and locked him up? And his only crime is having been born in Germany? Why would Maman want to help you?'

Major Ellis raised his hands as if faced by a raging tigress. 'Marius's arrest was nothing to do with me. This is the first day of the war. The whole country is in chaos. We have to follow the plans we've had for five years… and interning German-born people is just part of that plan.'

'But Marius hates the Nazis,' Aimee said. 'You heard me tell that to the sergeant. He left Germany as soon as Herr Hitler started to preach his hatred. He came to France, he married me, and we moved to Britain. Brigit has grown up here. He doesn't want to see Germany invade and march into Castle Bromwich. In fact, he's just the sort of person the Germans would execute if they ever landed.'

Again, Major Ellis raised his hands. 'We know, Aimee, we know. And I will make sure he's released as soon as the storms of war have died down. I'll talk to Mr Churchill himself, if I have to. It may take a month or so, but he'll be free, I promise.'

'You know Mr Churchill?' Brigit asked quietly. 'They say he'll be Prime Minister before the end of the year.'

Major Ellis nodded. 'It is likely. But he has been planning for this war for years. He has a top-secret plan that's going into action right now. And you, Aimee, are one of the first people we want for his new team.'

Aimee blinked. 'Mr Churchill knows about me?'

Major Ellis blew out his cheeks. 'Of course he does. You are a hero for what you did in the last war. You didn't get medals and reports in the newspapers, but the people in power know what you did back then and they need your help again.'

'Because she was so brave in the Great War?' Brigit asked.

'No, because she is French,' the officer said with a faint smile.

Chapter Seven

'We need a new way of fighting them'

Major Ellis looked at Brigit. 'Young lady, what I have to say to your maman is so secret I can't really share it with you. Would you be able to go somewhere else for half an hour? Maybe pack a case for your evacuation?'

'No,' Brigit said flatly. 'I don't want to be evacuated and I want to know what you're asking Maman to do.'

The major's mouth opened but he struggled to find words.

'Brigit, you can't speak like that to the major,' Aimee sighed.

'You always told me to stand up for myself...'

'Yes, but...'

'And say what I think.'

'Yes, I meant...'

'And not to let *anyone* make me do what I don't want to do. You said that's what made you grow up strong and I should be like you.'

The major shrugged. 'She sounds like a girl I knew back in France in 1918,' he said. 'Stay, Brigit. But only if you promise never to breathe a word of what you hear.'

'I swear on Billy Anderson's life,' she promised.

'Who's Billy Anderson?'

'The boy who threw a brick through our window,' Brigit said with her sweetest smile.

'Behave, Brigit,' Aimee murmured then turned to Major Ellis. 'I trust her. What can I do for you?'

The major poured himself another cup of tea. 'It's a shame you don't have any milk,' he said.

'No. The milkman has stopped delivering to us. I think it's because Marius is German.'

The major looked at her sharply. 'Broken windows and tradesmen refusing to serve you? It sounds as if it would be good for you to get away from Castle Bromwich.'

'Probably,' agreed Aimee.

'I am no longer in the army... though I still call myself a major. Ten years ago, I joined the British SIS... the Secret Intelligence Service.'

'I've never heard of it,' said Aimee.

Brigit rolled her eyes. 'That's the whole point, Maman. It's secret.'

Her mother blushed a little and muttered, 'Sorry.'

'We are spies. We've been finding out the enemy's secrets: their new weapons, the factories where they make their weapons and where their important bridges and power stations and railway links are. The idea was that if the war came...'

'Which it has,' Brigit put in.

'Which it has... then the Royal Air Force would know where to drop our bombs.'

'You've had spies finding all this out and sending it back to Britain?' Aimee asked.

'We have – and it was dangerous work. If they'd been caught – even before we went to war – the Nazi secret police, the Gestapo, would have arrested them and they'd never have been seen again. No trial, just torture then execution.'

'I don't see why the SIS needs me,' Aimee said softly.

'Ah, that's because Germany has blitzed Poland and our spies have told us they will head south to invade France next. We're pretty sure the French army isn't strong enough to stop them. The German army will march in and take over.'

'Like they did in the last war?' Brigit asked.

'Exactly. We'll send our soldiers across the English Channel to help the French, of course, but Mr Hitler has spent ten years building up a terrible force of armies attacking with tanks and bombers. We need a new way of fighting them.'

'Like the White Lady secret agents Grand-maman Colette worked with?' Brigit asked.

Major Ellis nodded. 'The White Lady told us where the German armies were and how strong they were. We want a new group to do more.' Brigit and her mother stayed silent, waiting. 'We want a secret army of French people to fight the invaders from the inside.'

Aimee shook her head. 'The White Lady spied, but we weren't an army. We couldn't pick up guns and fight the German tanks and dive-bombers. We wouldn't have lasted five minutes.'

'No one would ask the secret army to fight in that way. But if the Germans want telephone lines, the secret army can cut the wires. The enemy can guard every telegraph pole if they like – millions of them – but then they won't have enough men left to fight the war. The secret army would be ordinary French men and women, working during the day and turning to sabotage at night. We will provide the weapons, the explosives, the wireless sets and the leaders they need. They will be proud to fight for their country against the invaders.'

Aimee took a deep breath. 'And you want me to be one of the leaders? You want me to go back to France and wreck the German war machine?'

Major Ellis nodded.

'Why pick Maman?' Brigit asked.

'If we drop a British agent into France, the French may not like it. They are a proud people.

47

And the agent may give themselves away because they don't speak perfect French. Your mother knows the area around Bray as well as anyone. Your grandmother still lives there.'

Brigit gave a slight smile. 'When do we start?'

The adults looked at her. 'You will be evacuated to Wales, Brigit. There will be no one here to look after you.'

'Maman can look after me when we go to France. My French-speaking is perfect too. And no Gestapo men will suspect a woman with a daughter.'

The major blew out his cheeks again. 'Your mother's not going to France straightaway. She needs to spend the coming months training. How to fight with just her fists or maybe a knife. She needs to learn how to work the radios, to send us messages in code, to plant bombs and learn all the tricks of our top spies. Sorry, Brigit, Mr Churchill says the SOE won't be ready to start till enough of them have been trained, even if the Germans invade France tomorrow.'

'What's the SOE?'

'The Special Operations Executive... his name for the secret army.'

Brigit gave a single nod. 'Okay. But if I let myself get evacuated to Wales, will you promise to let me see Maman before she goes?'

Major Ellis was silent for a long while. 'I shall do my best. I can do no more.' He spoke briskly. 'Now, Brigit, you must prepare for evacuation. And Aimee, get ready to go to the secret SOE training camp.'

'Where are you sending her?' Brigit asked.

'It's a secret,' the major replied with a grin.

Chapter Eight

'She wants me to tell them you're my sister'

Monday, 4 September 1939: Castle Bromwich, England

The line of schoolchildren wound its way towards the railway station with a lot of noise. Teachers snapped at their pupils to stay off the road and to stop snivelling. 'Think of it as a great adventure,' a red-eyed Miss Dennison said. 'How many of you have been to the countryside before?'

About a quarter of the children raised their hands. 'And how many of you have been to Wales?' Most of the hands dropped. 'It's famous for its sheep.'

'Please, miss,' John Archbold said. 'Last term you said it was famous for its dragons and you told us the story of the dragon that kidnapped a princess and chained it to a rock.'

'A dragon is *not* going to mistake *you* for a princess, Archbold.'

'No, but that was just a trick by the dragon. It wanted the princess's dad to send a common boy or girl for it to eat every day or it would eat the princess, so the king did and we're common and...'

'Archbold, if you had listened to the end of the story you'd have known the dragon was killed by Saint George and he set the princess free.'

'Yes, miss, but there must be other dragons. I mean he can't have been the only dragon in Wales.'

Miss Dennison's face turned as purple-pink as her peppered eyes. 'Archbold. There. Are. No. Child-eating. Dragons. In. Wales. Only *sheep*.'

'What about if the dragons eat all the sheep? They'll come after us then,' John Archbold said, and a shiver of fear ran down the line.

'Enough about dragons,' Miss Dennison roared. 'You will walk in silence from now on.'

But the teacher couldn't order the parents to be silent. A few had come with their children to wave them goodbye.

The wise parents told their children how much fun they would have. The foolish parents sobbed and told their sons and daughters how much they would miss them and that set their children off crying.

Brigit Furst had no parent with her. Her dad was in the camp that had been quickly built on the Hodgehill golf course and her maman was already on a train that was heading to the SOE training camp.

As the snaking line of pupils reached the road past Castle Bromwich Hall, a line of children from Hodgehill School joined them. The road took a long loop around the great gardens of the hall. Army lorries were smoking and roaring along the road then turning into the gardens. 'More dangerous than a smoking roaring dragon,' Brigit thought.

'They're using the hall as a store now that old Lady Ida's dead,' Billy Anderson said. 'The place'll be full of stuff. If I wasn't being evacuated I bet I could rob the place and make a fortune.'

'I bet you could,' Brigit said. 'Wouldn't help us win the war, though.'

'No. Maybe not. But it'd help me and Mum get through,' Billy argued.

They walked on and the pupils from the other school began to mingle. Suddenly Brigit almost stumbled over a girl who'd stopped to tie her shoelaces. The girl looked up. 'Brigit,' she said.

'Jessie?'

'I have to speak to you. In secret,' the thin girl squeaked. The two dropped back in the line till there was no one near them.

'Listen, Brigit, Gladys Turnbull has a plot to get you.'

'She's had a plot to get me ever since I came to Castle Bromwich,' Brigit said. 'But I'm still here. I'm not scared of her.'

'I know. But she can make your life really nasty when we get excavated.'

'Evacuated.'

'Yes, that an' all. She wants me to stick with you. When we get to the other end there'll be people

53

there to give us a home. She wants me to tell them you're my sister and we want to be kept together. In the same house, like.'

'We have different names. I'm Furst and you're Burdess.'

'Gladys has thought of that. She says I'm to say we're step-sisters – same mum, different dad.'

'And how will that help her plot to get me?'

'She won't,' Jessie moaned. 'I'll be the one to do it.'

Brigit blinked. 'Thanks for warning me. But how?'

'Listen. These people that give us homes think us city kids are dirty and full of fleas and never take a bath and don't know what a toilet is. They think we're so mucky we wet the bed… and they won't have that. They make bed-wetters sleep on the floor, Gladys says.'

'But I don't wet the bed,' Brigit said with a puzzled smile.

'That's why I have to take a cup of water and pour it on your sheets.'

'Why is it a problem? You just don't do it.'

The thin girl moaned. 'Because we'll all end up in the same school, probably. If *I* don't get *you* in our new house, then Gladys says *she'll* get *me* in the classroom. At break. She'll take scissors and cut off my hair. She'll twist my arm till I can't write. She'll jam my head through railings and leave me to starve to death. It's all part of her wicked plan.'

Brigit shook her head. 'If Gladys can make plans, then so can I. Don't worry, Jessie, you won't have to wet my bed.'

Jessie gave a scared grin. 'I knew you'd think of something.'

Brigit wrapped an arm round the thin girl's shoulders and gave her a hug. 'Thanks for telling me, Jess. It took a lot of courage. Now, this is what we're going to do.' She whispered in Jessie's ear and the girl nodded.

They hurried on and joined the back of the Hodgehill School line.

Chapter Nine

'The early worm catches the train'

The pupils reached the bridge over the River Tame and looked across the water. The old rubber factory stood prison-grey and ugly to their left. Ahead the aeroplane factory was swarming with workers like ants. The bomb shelters for the workers, in fresh red brick, stood out.

To their right the new Castle Bromwich airfield was being finished with smart tarmac runways and hangars. An orange wind sock showed there was a breeze from the south-west.

A fighter plane with curved wings was pulled out of a hangar by the air crew and the propeller blade stuttered into action then whirred and roared.

The pupils and the teachers and parents stopped to watch as it trundled down the runway to the far end. It turned so the nose was facing into the breeze and rolled ever faster towards the river side of the airfield. It leaped into the air, over the heads of the evacuees and its wheels were tucked up into its wings.

The children cheered and waved their hats and caps. Someone said the pilot waved back. An excited Hodgehill boy told Brigit, 'They're going to use this airfield to test the Spitfires from the factory before they set out to fight the war in the air.'

His teacher, an older woman with grey hair set in fixed waves, spoke sharply. 'Quiet, Fred. You never know who may be listening. If the Germans find out this is one of our Spitfire factories they'll bomb it. Careless talk costs lives.'

'Sorry, Miss South,' Fred muttered, blushing.

The teacher's lined face softened. 'Don't worry, Fred, I don't think there are any Germans within a thousand miles of here. Just be careful in future.'

A girl with spectacles that were two perfect circles shuffled close to Brigit. She wore a fawn coat over her white blouse and grey skirt, white knee socks and black shoes. The Hodgehill uniforms looked just like Brigit's and she was sure her plan would work.

The spectacled girl smiled and said, 'Those Spitfires are going to stop the Blitz, my dad says.' She peered more closely at Brigit. 'I haven't seen you in school before, have I?'

'No, I'm Brigit... Hurst.'

'I'm Jean Mason. Are you new this term?'

'That's right. Today was supposed to be my first day. I haven't even told Miss South I'm here. I was in such a rush to join the evacuees' line.'

'Oh, Miss South will be fine about it. She's lovely is Miss South.' Jean lowered her voice and said, 'We're just lucky to go to Hodgehill. You won't believe the teachers they have in Castle Bromwich School. They're terrors, I heard.'

'Bad teachers?' Brigit asked, hiding a smile.

'No, cruel bullies. I heard about one boy called Charlie – the head teacher hit his hand with a cane. Snapped it clean in two.'

'What? His hand?'

'No-o-o. The cane, silly.' Jean laughed. 'I'm glad our school's not like that.'

Brigit nodded. 'I suppose I should go and see Miss South and get registered or something.'

'Let me go with you. I can be your first friend in the school,' Jean offered.

'Thanks, Jean.'

The girls elbowed their way through other Hodgehill pupils to find the teacher who was trying to answer a dozen questions at once. 'No, James, sheep don't bite... yes, Janet, the Welsh people will feed you, and you won't have to wait for food parcels from home... you may live on a farm, Peter, but you won't be sleeping in a chicken shed... Now, who have we here?' she asked, looking at Brigit.

'Excuse me, Miss South, I was told to report to you this morning, but my dad had trouble finding Hodgehill School. By the time we got there you were on your way to the station.'

'The early worm catches the train,' the teacher said and gave a light laugh at her own joke. 'But why would you want to see me at the school?'

'You should have received a letter last week? From the Royal Air Force?' Brigit said.

Miss South's face was blank. 'They want me to be a pilot?'

'No. My dad is a Spitfire pilot in… a secret airbase in East Anglia.'

'So he doesn't need me to be a pilot? He can do it?' the teacher teased.

'He's been transferred to Castle Bromwich airfield, to be a test pilot,' Brigit went on, nodding towards the field across the river. 'I had to leave the… secret airbase in East Anglia. I was supposed to start at Hodgehill School today. But with the war…'

'Ah yes, the war.'

'So can I be evacuated with your school… please?'

Miss South frowned. 'I suppose so. I'm sure all the paperwork will catch up later.'

There was a stirring among the school groups as Castle Bromwich School led the way down the long ramp to the station platform. In the distance, a plume of white smoke showed a train huffing towards them. Brigit hung back as Miss South herded her children like ducks towards the platform. She made sure the teacher was walking between her and Miss Dennison's Castle Bromwich pupils and kept her head low.

As she slipped past she heard Jessie Burdess explain, 'Brigit Furst's mother said she'd changed her mind. She doesn't want Brigit to be evacuated.'

'Tsch,' Miss Dennison snorted. 'We're better off without the sour kraut. Stand back from the platform edge, Castle Bromwich pupils. We take this first train. If you fall on the railway line, we'll all be held up while they clear the mess off the tracks. Stand back, Billy Anderson... do *not* answer me back. There'll be a cane waiting for you in Wales, you mark my words.'

As her old schoolmates boarded the train, Brigit smiled the smile of an escaped prisoner.

Chapter Ten

'It's a dangerous job'

A train pulled into the station. A small black locomotive pulling some ancient coaches that had once been coloured brown or dark red, green or cream, but now showed grimy wood where the paint was peeling away. The steam from the engine rained down soot on to the platform. Tear-choked children from Castle Bromwich turned and waved to their parents who stood on the bridge over the track.

White and dirty-white handkerchiefs were waved and were used to smother sobs and sniffles of misery. Miss Dennison split her classes into groups of eight – one group for each compartment. There were arguments as friends were separated. 'You'll see them at the other end – it's only a couple of hours,' the teacher snapped.

At last they were loaded and the teacher nodded to the station-master. He waved a green flag at the driver and Miss Dennison lit a cigarette before climbing into the guard's van at the back. The sobs of the parents became wails. Then children crowded to the windows for a final glimpse of their home town and their parents.

The train creaked and the carriages clattered on their couplings as slowly it pulled away from the platform. Jessie Burdess's pale face looked across at Brigit and she gave a faint smile. Brigit gave a thumbs-up and mouthed the words, 'Good luck, Jessie. See you soon.'

But Brigit would never see Jessie again.

*

A whistle sounded a mile away as the next evacuee train gave the signal it was ready to pull into the station. Brigit's new teacher, Miss South, guided her class into groups of eight. 'I'll try to keep friends together as far as I can,' she promised.

'There are no parents to say goodbye,' Brigit said.

The teacher shook her head. 'They said goodbye at the school gates. I thought it would be less upsetting for everyone.' They watched the Castle Bromwich parents drift back from the bridge to the town, still sniffling and wiping teary eyes. 'Now, Brigit, I don't suppose you've made any friends yet?'

Jean Mason stepped forward. 'I'll look after her,' she offered.

'Thank you, Jean,' the teacher said warmly. She peered through her glasses at Brigit's label. 'Now, Jean, this is Brigit Furst.'

'No,' Brigit said quickly. 'I think the lady in the school office got my label wrong. It should be Brigit *Hurst*.'

'Ah, that makes sense,' Miss South said. 'I can't imagine a Spitfire pilot with a German name. It would be like having our prime minister called Fritz Chamberlain.' She chuckled at her own joke and turned to watch the train draw near to the station with hisses of steam and grating creaks on the rails.

Some of the children near Brigit left their group. One of the boys with Brian Bellamy on his label said, 'Is that right? Your dad's a Spitfire pilot? Has he shot down any Germans?'

Brigit knew she was going to have to keep up the lie she'd started. 'He's a test pilot – across the road at the factory. You probably saw him fly over just now.'

'That was your dad?' Brian asked and his jaw fell to his chest.

'Who did you think he was waving at?'

'He was waving at all of us,' a boy labelled Michael Purdy said.

'Is that what you think?' Brigit said coyly as the train rattled to a halt beside them.

'You mean…' Brian asked.

Brigit smiled and shrugged, then picked up her suitcase so she didn't have to go on with her tale.

'Have you flown with him?' Michael asked. 'I've always wanted to fly in a Spitfire.'

Brigit was wise enough to avoid that trap. 'A Spitfire only has one seat. If I sat on Dad's knee he wouldn't be able to see where he was going. Anyway, he is *testing* new ideas – that's why he's called a test pilot. Some of them may go wrong so it's a dangerous job.'

Brian and Michael nodded wisely as they allowed themselves to be herded towards their carriages by the station-master. 'Excuse me, young sirs, but were you thinking of travelling today? Because the driver is running out of coal waiting for you,' he said.

Michael Purdy stuck out his tongue at the station-master just as Miss South turned to the group. 'Michael Purdy, that is very rude. Apologise at once to the gentleman.'

'Sorry, sir,' Michael mumbled. 'Brian Bellamy told me to do it.'

'You liar,' Brian exploded. 'Please, miss, don't believe the little rat. I never…'

'You and Michael had better travel in separate compartments,' the teacher said.

'Awwww,' the boys moaned together.

'But he's my best friend,' Michael argued.

'He can come in our compartment, miss,' Jean Mason said, and Brian glared at her.

'Thank you, Jean,' said Miss South. 'You are like my mother hen today, looking after Brigit and now Brian. In you get. Put your gas masks on the

66

rack above your heads and don't forget them when you get out at the other end.'

They climbed aboard and settled into their seats. Some girls pulled out comics like *The Dandy* and started to read about Desperate Dan and his huge appetite for cow pie. Jean began to read the adventures of Korky the Cat, but Brigit had a book called *War of the Worlds*.

'What's that about?' Brian asked. 'I never read a book before. We don't have books in our house. Just beer bottles.'

'The Earth is invaded by creatures from Mars. They have three-legged fighting machines with heat rays and poisonous black smoke.'

'Wow. I hope the people on Earth had their gas masks with them,' Jean gasped.

'They wouldn't work against the heat-ray guns,' Brigit explained. 'The Martian monsters just fried the humans to a crisp.'

'That's like the German flame-throwers in the last war.' Brian nodded. 'That's what'll happen if the Germans land here.'

Brigit closed the book. 'We'll have to make sure that never happens then.'

'We can't do anything to stop them.' Jean sighed. 'Not us kids.'

'Maybe you can't,' Brigit murmured. 'But maybe I can.'

Chapter Eleven

'How will we know where we are when we get there?'

The train seemed to shuffle along the track for a few miles, then it would stop at a signal. It stood there, steaming, for what seemed like no reason at all. Then it shuffled off again.

After a couple of hours it pulled into a small station – no more than a platform – and Miss South called for them all to get out of their carriages. 'Sorry this is taking so long. There are lots of our soldiers and sailors and airmen moving around the country to defend us. They are more important than us, so we must keep stopping to let their trains go through. While we are here, use the station toilets, and if you have any spare sandwiches and bottles of pop, share them with those who haven't any, please.'

The children settled on the grassy bank beside the platform and unpacked sandwich packets and bottles from their suitcases. A station-worker was painting out the name boards with whitewash. 'Why is he doing that?' Brian Bellamy asked.

'The Germans may send soldiers across on parachutes,' Miss South explained. 'They'll have maps but they won't know exactly where they have landed. We don't want to make it easy for them so we're taking down road signs and painting out place names like these.'

'Then how will we know where we are when we get there?' Jean asked.

'We'll know,' the teacher said, but she didn't look too sure.

Steam hissed, the children ate quietly, and birds hurried across the sky going about their lives as usual. Blackbirds sang in a distant wood and small clouds drifted across the warm September sky.

Brian looked up at the emptiness. 'It doesn't feel like there's a war on, does it?'

Then a faint white line was scratched on the cornflower-blue sky as an aeroplane flew high to the east. 'We'll know about it soon enough when the bombers come,' Brigit said.

The peace was broken when the train driver gave a blast of his whistle to signal that the line was clear and they were ready to move again. A station porter who looked a hundred years old collected their wrappers and empty bottles in sacks. 'Now we're at war we mustn't waste a thing – not a scrap of paper or a single glass bottle,' Brigit said.

'Or food,' Jean added. 'There's going to be a law against wasting food, my mum says. The women in her factory even have a poster with a little poem about it.' She went on to recite it while the children stopped to listen.

'Auntie threw her ham away,
To the lock-up she was taken.
There she is and there she'll stay,
Till she learns to save her bacon.'

The children of Hodgehill School smiled and clapped. If any of them were still upset at leaving home, they didn't show it now. 'I'm glad I came with you,' Brigit said.

Jean grinned and tucked Brigit's hand under her arm as they walked back to their carriage. 'It's lovely to have you. It feels like we've been friends for years.'

Brigit just nodded and climbed inside. As the train pulled away Brian pulled out a mouth organ and began to play in time with the clicking of the wheels on the rails.

'I know that song,' a girl said and began to sing. By the end, the whole carriage was joining in and the blackbirds seemed to stop and listen.

'I'll say a prayer while I am gone;
I'll pray each night, and pray each morn;
Though we're apart, we're not alone,
We'll live to share a peaceful dawn.'

If the words made the children a little mournful then Brian slapped a hand on his *Beano* comic. 'Look at this joke... I say! I say! Where does Hitler keep his armies?'

'Don't know,' the others said together. 'Where does Hitler keep his armies?'

'Up his sleevies,' the boy laughed.

And they shuffled along all afternoon as the cornflower-blue sky turned to purple velvet. At last the train pulled in to a platform that was lit by railway lamps and where a row of adults with serious faces stood silent and still, waiting.

'I think this is it,' Brigit said. 'Miss South said we'd know when we get here.'

'What do they want?' Jean asked.

'They want to take us off to their homes – our *new* homes,' Brigit said.

'But how do we know which homes we go to?'

'I think they line us up and they get to pick the ones they want.'

'Oh no,' Brian Bellamy groaned. 'It's like when we pick football teams in the schoolyard. I'm always left till last.'

Brigit laughed. 'That's what Billy Anderson always says.'

The others in the carriage stopped and looked at her. 'Who's Billy Anderson?'

No one could see Brigit's ears turn red and her mouth twist awkwardly. 'Just someone I used to know.'

'In your last school?' Jean asked.

Brigit was saved by Miss South who was walking along the platform and opening the doors. 'Do *not* forget to take your gas masks. You may not need them in Wales, but you mustn't lose them.'

'Is that where we are, Miss South? In Wales?'

'That's what the ticket collector told me, now out you all get.'

The children climbed down under the stern gazes of the waiting adults and huddled together like sheep surrounded by wolves.

Miss South spoke. 'Now, I know you're all very tired, but this is the last part of the journey. Could I ask you to line up against the station buildings here, please?'

The wary, wide-eyed children moved over to the cluster of waiting rooms, ticket office, porter's room and luggage room.

A man stepped forward and startled everyone by raising his hands in the air, as if he were shooing chickens out of his garden. He was pale in the light of the lanterns and large ears stuck out from his long head. 'Welcome to Aberpont, my young friends. Welcome. *I* am the Reverend Hywel *Williams* and the *leader* of the local *chapel*.' His voice went up and down like his thick grey eyebrows. He stretched out his arms in a wide scarecrow welcome. 'We have *prayed* for your safe arrival and *here* you are. God is *good* and he hath *delivered* you from the *tormenting* fire of *war* to our piece of *heaven* here on *Earth*.'

Brian Bellamy sighed quietly. 'What a nutter.'

The Reverend Williams walked down the line of children as the other adults stood silent. It seemed the Reverend had first pick. He stopped when he reached Brigit. 'I'll take you,' he said with a grin that showed crooked teeth.

'I have to stay with my cousin here,' Brigit said grabbing Jean Mason by the sleeve.

The man blew out his cheeks. 'I suppose I can take you both if you don't mind sharing a bed?'

Jean nodded happily and they set off into the darkening village after their new guardian.

Chapter Twelve

'You have a lot of goodness in Wales'

Tuesday, 14 May 1940: Aberpont, Wales

The girls had been there over eight months and they were growing used to the Reverend Williams's strange ways. The Reverend sat at the breakfast table and prayed. Jean and Brigit bowed their heads and tried not to giggle. 'Oh Lord, we thank you for giving us our daily *bread* and we *ask* you, dear Father, to *bless* it with your holy spirit so it may *live* within us for the rest of the *day*, or at least until we next *eat* some blessed meal.'

'Amen,' the girls muttered and reached for the toast. But the man hadn't finished.

'And we ask that *Brigit* and *Jean* learn well at school and learn their *maths* and *history* and *geography* well, but that they learn their *scriptures* best of all.'

'Amen.'

'And that they try harder with their *Welsh* lessons and learn to speak God's own language like a *native*.' He looked up and nodded at Brigit.

'Oh. Yes. Amen,' she said.

'Amen, indeed.' He smiled. 'Now, girls, today the village received the latest sack of letters from *England*.' He went to the sideboard to collect two envelopes and handed one to each girl.

Jean began to tear hers open but the Reverend Williams said sharply, 'Not at the breakfast table, Jean. Wait until you are walking to school.'

'But it's raining,' the girl sighed.

'God is sending the rain to *water* the earth, the flowers and the trees. Rain is *good*.'

'You have a lot of goodness in Wales then, don't you?' Brigit said sweetly.

'God's own country is indeed *blessed*.' He nodded. 'Now eat up. Build your *strength* for your day at school. *Sing* your hearts out in the school *assembly*.'

'They sing in Welsh,' Jean said. 'We don't understand it.'

'All the more reason for you to work *hard* at your *Welsh* lessons,' he said.

The girls ate in silence. The old cook brought bacon, sausage and eggs on fried bread from the kitchen and placed it in front of the Reverend. The girls ate toast. 'This food is on ration,' he explained as egg yolk ran down his chin. 'That means everyone is only allowed so much food each week. It will be hard, but we must all suffer a little if we are going to win the war.'

'Some of us suffer more than others,' Brigit said looking from her toast to the man's greasy plate. 'Where is our bacon and egg?'

'Adults need *more* food than children,' the man said as he forked half a sausage between his twisted teeth. He sighed. 'I remember the days when we used to have *tomatoes* with my breakfast. No *tomatoes* at the village shop, Mrs Davies?'

'None left yesterday, sir.'

'Maybe get there *earlier* today. Get to the *front* of the queue. Tell Mr Jones Shop who it's *for*.'

'I tried that yesterday,' she muttered.

'And what did he say?'

'He said he had no tomatoes, and if Jesus himself walked into the shop he'd still have no tomatoes. Not unless Jesus turned the old potatoes into tomatoes the way he turned the water into wine.'

The Reverend's face went dark. 'I shall have to have a *word* with Mr Jones Shop,' he snapped. 'Now, girls, clean your *teeth* and get off to *school*.'

They rose from the table, gathered their letters and went to fetch the paper carrier bags they used to carry their schoolbooks, pencils and pens.

The drizzle wet Brigit's hair and ran down the back of her neck. They hung up their coats in the cloakroom but were called into the assembly hall before they had a chance to read their letters.

After a small lunch of greasy lamb stew with lumpy mashed potato and tasteless cabbage they found they had five minutes to themselves. Brigit opened her letter and read eagerly. The flap opened easily – as if someone had already steamed it open and read it. She had known for a while that the Reverend Williams liked to stick his pointed nose into her letters.

Her mother had written every week since September. But this letter was a puzzle.

Brigit knew her mother's writing well and she always told her daughter to write small but neatly so she didn't waste any paper. Aimee Furst had written on schoolbook paper with faint lines. But she wrote on a line then left a blank line. She finished a whole page the same way. On the second page she only wrote two lines and left the rest of the page empty. And the message was odd too.

Dearest Brigit,

I hope your evacuation is still a happy and healthy time for you. Keep writing to me at our old address and it will be sent on to me as I travel around Britain. As you know I am training to do war work, but I cannot tell you anything about it. It is top secret and if an enemy spy opens this letter we will have betrayed our countries.

I can tell you that your father is doing fine and hopes to be back at work next month. They are treating him well.

I am working with some of the bravest men and women you could ever wish to meet. I am learning new skills – most of them that I cannot tell you about. But there is one that I can share as it is not a great secret and you may find it is fun. On the other hand, you may not be able to buy lemons so you won't be able to try it.

Brigit scratched her head. This didn't sound at all like her mother writing. But she carried on reading...

I was told to squeeze some lemon juice into a bowl and add a little water and write with it. You can't see a word, but when you hold the paper in front of a warm candle it appears like magic. It's invisible ink. Great fun. You must try it some time.

As you will know from the radio news, France has been invaded. That means my serious work is likely to begin soon and I may be out of touch for a while.

I hope you like this scented paper.
Love,
Maman

Scented paper? As the school bell rang to call the children to their lessons Brigit held the letter to her nose and sniffed. It smelled of lemons. She smiled and knew what her mother wanted her to do.

Chapter Thirteen

'Blood, toil, tears and sweat'

That night in the cold bed with the rusting iron bedstead, Brigit read a book and waited till Jean fell asleep. It had been an evening of bad temper and argument.

After a supper of fried fish, the Reverend had switched on the radio to listen to the news. 'Holland has surrendered to the German army,' he said.

Brigit had heard that and didn't need him to repeat it as if he were speaking to simpletons. '*Britain* will be next,' he went on.

'I think Belgium then France will be next,' Brigit said. She almost added, 'My mother's homeland,' then remembered she was supposed to be Brigit Hurst from Hodgehill near Castle Bromwich with a father who tested Spitfires.

Reverend Williams looked annoyed. 'Yes, yes, but they are as good as gone *already*. The British army is being driven back to the *sea* and then there will be nothing to *stop* Herr Hitler from invading.'

'The radio said there was a new army being formed to defend Britain. The Local Defence Volunteers,' Jean added. 'They'll stop the Germans.'

The man sighed. 'A Home *Guard*. Made up of all the *sweepings* of old folks' homes and schools – the ones too *old* or too *young* to fight properly. No, let us put our faith in *God* and not the LDV.'

'Amen,' Jean said.

Brigit was cross at the man's defeatist words. 'Mr Churchill's our prime minister now. He says we won't be giving up.' She picked up the paper. 'Haven't you read what he said yesterday?' Brigit began to read. 'We are in one of the greatest battles in history. The air battle goes on…'

'Your dad flying Spitfires.' Jean nodded.

'Many preparations have to be made here at home,' Brigit went on reading.

'The Home Guard,' Jean said to the Reverend Williams, as if he were the simpleton now.

Brigit raised her voice till she sounded like a young Churchill. The cook came to listen from the kitchen. *'I have nothing to offer but blood, toil, tears and sweat. We have before us many, many long months of struggle and of suffering. You ask, what is our policy? I will say: It is to wage war, by sea, land and air, with all our might and with all the strength that God can give us.'*

'Amen,' Jean and the cook cried together.

Brigit's voice grew stronger. *'To wage war against a monstrous tyranny. That is our policy. You ask, what is our aim? I can answer in one word: Victory. Victory at all costs – Victory in spite of all terror – Victory, however long and hard the road may be, for without victory there is no survival.'*

Brigit waved the newspaper towards the Reverend as Jean and Cook cheered. 'My God will be with me,' the old woman cried.

'Then I hope he's wearing a bulletproof jacket,' the Reverend snarled. He rose to his feet and slammed a fist on the table. 'The Germans *cannot* be stopped. When they march down the main street of Aberpont I shall *meet* them and make our *peace*. Now get to bed, you girls, and let me hear no more *nonsense* about Home Guards or Churchill or stopping the invasion. As God is my witness, it cannot be *done*. Get to bed. And you, Alice,' he finished pointing to the cook, 'get back to your *kitchen* and serve me my treacle pudding.'

The girls went to bed as hungry as ever. Now Brigit pulled the candle towards her and held her mother's letter close enough to the flame to let it warm the lemon ink. The words began to appear, and Brigit read what Aimee really wanted to say.

Please burn this once you have read it. What I say is secret. Top secret.

When Major Ellis told me that he had a special task for me he was not able to tell me much about what it was. That was the first part of the four-part training. First, we were tested to see if we were the right sort of person they needed – but they didn't tell us what *we were needed for. Some dropped out, but I went on to a Group A school in Scotland. There we were taught fighting skills – using weapons like guns and knives. We learned something called judo – how to fight without weapons no matter how big your enemy might be. We learned how to make and plant bombs. Then it was down to Manchester to learn how to parachute. You would laugh because we dropped with a small spade fastened to a leg. Can you guess why? It's so we can bury the parachute after we land. We went on to the New Forest in the south where they taught us about working a radio to send signals in code. There doesn't seem to be any end to what we need to know. Map-reading and using a compass and simply staying alive in the wild. You have told me about the Reverend Williams. He'd be shocked if he knew we were taught how to pick locks and become burglars.*

You know Major Ellis told you that this was Mr Churchill's idea. He wants to create his Special Operations Executive or SOE. But what that really means is spies and saboteurs – wreckers. I have passed all the tests and that is why I am writing to you. As soon as Mr Churchill decides the time is right, I will be flown across there, dropped by parachute and set about my work. I'll be dropped near Bray-on-Somme near where Grand-maman lives because I know the area so well.

Major Ellis has kept his promise and has arranged for me to see you before I go. I have one last piece of training to finish. It is working with miniature submarines at a camp near Fishguard Bay in Pembrokeshire. The bus will stop so that I can visit you as I travel through Wales at the end of May.

Take care of yourself, my love, and don't let that preacher make your life miserable. The war can't go on forever. We shall all be together one day. Stay strong.

Love,

Maman

Brigit choked back tears. Then she shook her head. 'Stop being a baby,' she muttered to herself. 'You know what you have to do? Yes. Then start planning. Start planning right now.'

Her plan was almost complete when she drifted into a deep sleep.

Chapter Fourteen

'Maybe he doesn't wear socks'

Tuesday, 28 May 1940: Aberpont, Wales

Two weeks later, Brigit was ready to put her plan into action.

On the day, the girls were up with the dawn. Reverend Williams said they had to keep their room spotless. 'As the great Methodist preacher John Wesley said in one of his sermons: "Slovenliness is no part of religion. Cleanliness is indeed next to Godliness." So you will clean your room before you leave it every morning. And then you can clean the dining room so I don't have to eat breakfast in the mouse-filth that the wicked creatures leave every night.'

Brigit cleaned the room eagerly, knowing her plan was settled. Jean was slow as ever. 'If Reverend Williams is so clean then why doesn't he change his socks?' she asked.

'Maybe he doesn't wear socks,' Brigit said in mock amazement. 'Maybe he just has grey ankles because he doesn't wash his feet.' The girls giggled, picked up their school bags and gas masks and hurried downstairs to sweep the mouse-droppings off the table then gather them from the floor.

Alice the cook placed porridge on the table for them then went back into the kitchen to fry the Reverend's breakfast. He appeared just as the servant placed his bacon, sausages, egg and fried bread on the table. The porridge cooled as they waited for him to bless their food. 'Tea?' he demanded.

'Just brewing in the pot, your reverence,' the old woman replied.

'Still no tomatoes, I see?' he sniffed.

'Sorry, sir. I told Mr Jones Shop you'd say an extra prayer for him, but he said he had none. I even offered to pay him, but he still had none.'

'That man gets no prayers from me,' the Reverend said, his face turning purple with anger. 'Or at least I will pray that his miserable soul goes straight to Hell and roasts on the Devil's hobs.'

'Can you roast a soul then?' Brigit asked quietly.

The Reverend glared at her. 'You will find out one day,' he hissed.

'Won't you find out first?' she asked politely. 'I mean, you'll probably die before me.'

'That may well be, but I will not be going straight to Hell,' he roared. 'I am not a sinner.'

'Wrath is one of the seven deadly sins, my teacher says,' Brigit said. 'What does wrath mean?'

'It means anger,' the Reverend raged, spitting crumbs of crisped bacon on to the table the girls had just polished. For a moment Brigit thought he was going to hit her. Instead he took a deep breath and said in a low voice, 'And it is lucky for you that I do not suffer from the sin of wrath.'

'Thank you, sir,' Brigit said with a sigh. Jean had begun to eat her watery porridge. 'Have we any sugar for the porridge, Reverend?' she asked. 'We always had sugar at home.'

The man looked at the sugar bowl on the table and placed two heaped spoonfuls in his teacup. 'Sugar is on ration,' he said calmly. 'There is scarcely enough for my tea. Our brave sailors must cross the Atlantic Ocean and risk being sunk by German submarines, just so we can have our sugar. You must learn to do without it. Every spoonful is probably a sailor's life saved.'

'My teacher said that another sin is gluttony, is that right?'

The man slammed his knife and fork on the table and his face was a deeper purple and his eyes bloodshot. 'Enough, child. Enough of your impertinence.' He raised his hand above his head and this time Brigit was sure he was going to strike her.

They were interrupted by a rattle at the front door. 'That'll be the post,' Alice said, shuffling from the kitchen.

'Then get it,' the Reverend snapped. He was breathing heavily and he snatched the letters from the servant when she returned.

He tore open the first envelope and pulled out a sheet of paper. It was blank. He stared at it for a moment then turned over the envelope. 'It's for you,' he said, throwing it on the table. 'Someone's idea of a joke,' he mumbled, but Brigit's heart leaped.

He looked more carefully at the second envelope. 'For you, Jean, dear child,' he said.

Jean beamed. 'I'll wait till I get to school to open it,' she promised.

But the Reverend Williams wasn't listening. He was frowning over the brown envelope in his hand. He turned it over and looked at his name and address, then at the back. Brigit noticed it was printed with the words 'On His Majesty's Service'.

'What does the king want with *me*?' he said, puzzled but pleased and self-important.

He tore open the top and pulled out a couple of pages of typed notepaper. His smug smile turned to a frown and then his face clouded with anger. He raised his eyes to Brigit but spoke to Jean. 'Get to *school*, Jean. I need to have a *word* with Brigit.'

Jean scooped the last of the porridge into her mouth before taking her plate to the kitchen.

She gathered up her school bag and gas mask then scuttled out of the door like one of the midnight mice.

The Reverend cleaned his plate and mopped up the grease with a piece of fresh white bread. Then he wiped his mouth against his sleeve and sat back in his chair. 'Follow me into my *study*,' he ordered and led the way into his private room. It was lined with books and smelled of tobacco and leather. He closed the door behind Brigit, turned the key in the lock and put it in his pocket.

The Reverend sat at his desk and pointed for Brigit to take the chair at the other side. He was trying to look stern, but Brigit could see he was going to enjoy whatever came next.

'Brigit,' he said finally.

'That's my name,' she agreed carefully.

'Brigit *what*?'

'Brigit Watt? No, Brigit Hurst.'

Reverend Williams gave a tight smile at her small joke then leaned forward. His breath smelled like bacon and acid. He looked at the letter again and began to read.

'*Dear Reverend Williams,*

I work for the government department that deals with evacuees. I understand you are the leader of the villagers hosting Birmingham children in Aberpont.

You were sent children from Hodgehill School, south of the River Tame. However, we believe there has been a mistake and that one of the children who arrived at Aberpont is in fact from the nearby Castle Bromwich School. We do not know if this was accidental or if it was planned.

I think you must not know about this mistake or you would have been in touch with us before now.'

The Reverend licked his lips and looked at Brigit who felt herself turning pale. He read on.

'*The name of the child is Brigit Furst.*'

And Brigit was sure she was going to faint.

Chapter Fifteen

'It's enough to make a saint swear'

The Reverend Williams raised his eyebrows and waited for Brigit to speak. Her throat was desert-dry and her tongue seemed stuck to the roof of her mouth. He carried on.

'In such cases we would leave the child where he or she is settled. However, Brigit Furst is half-German and her father is at present detained in an internment camp. Brigit Furst is probably not a risk to the security of Britain. We must nevertheless

keep her under close observation where she, and the country, will be safe.

A copy of this letter will be sent to the local constable. Please keep the girl in a secure place until he is able to detain her and return her to Castle Bromwich where the staff of her school will care for her since we have been unable to trace her mother.

Yours sincerely,

Edgar Bottomley – Evacuee Services.'

Reverend Williams put down the letter and tapped it with his thin and dirty finger. 'Your name is Brigit Hurst? *Liar*. Your father is a brave Spitfire test pilot? *Liar*. You are a pupil at Hodgehill School? *Liar*. We have already *talked* about what happens to *liars* when they die, *haven't* we? I spoke about it in my sermon in the chapel just the other Sunday. They go straight to Hell. There will be no Judgement Day for them, for they have already been found *guilty*.'

He rose slowly and walked to the door. He unlocked it, stepped through and locked it again from the outside. Brigit felt sick for a few minutes then decided that being sent back to Castle

Bromwich would be a disaster. What had the letter said? *The staff of her school will care for her.*

Would it be the spiteful Miss Dennison, if she'd returned from Wales? Maybe she would have learned from Gladys Turnbull how that pepper got into her eyes. Or the vicious Mr Cutter? Either would be misery every bit as cruel as the Reverend Williams' fires of Hell.

She sniffed and reached into the pocket of her dress for her handkerchief. She pulled out a piece of paper. It was the blank sheet that had been in the envelope Reverend Williams had opened at the breakfast table. There was an electric lamp on his desk and she turned it on. The bulb soon grew hot and she held the paper to it till writing appeared.

This time the letter from her mother was quite short.

Brigit. I will be passing through Aberpont at around noon on 28 May. I hope you can get out of school long enough to meet the bus, so we can say goodbye before I go to France. Love, Maman

Brigit nodded. That was always her escape plan but now she would be doing it while the police and the villagers of Aberpont were searching for a half-German girl who could be a traitor.

First, however, she had to get out of this locked room. She didn't have Maman's lock-picking and burglar skills. But maybe she didn't need them. She stepped over to the window and looked around the heavy curtain. A sweating policeman was walking slowly along the road and turned in at the gateway.

The catch on the window was stiff but she turned it then stepped back into the shadow of the dusty curtain until the policeman had knocked on the door. As soon as the door was opened by Alice the cook and the policeman stepped inside, Brigit knew she had just a minute to make her escape.

The catch was open, but the old window frame was warped by years of Welsh rain. It wouldn't move. Brigit looked around the room and saw a pair of candlesticks on the mantelpiece. She picked one up and used the heavy base to hammer at the handle to push it outwards without smashing the glass.

'I locked her in here, Constable Evans,' Reverend Williams was saying in the corridor outside.

'Very good, sir,' the policeman replied.

The girl gave one last desperate blow and the window creaked and swung open. She heard the key rattle in the lock. If she jumped out now they would see her run off and be able to follow. It was a small village with nowhere to hide.

The lock clicked open. 'I'll be glad to be rid of her.' The Reverend sighed. 'Cheeky, cunning brat.'

Brigit looked at his desk. Anyone sitting there sat between two stacks of drawers with the leather-covered desktop over them. Between the drawers there was a space where the knees went. Brigit dived for that and made herself as small as she could. It smelled of feet and the dust made her want to sneeze.

The Reverend stepped into the room and swore. 'Hell's teeth.'

'I beg your pardon, your reverence,' the shocked policeman rumbled.

'Sorry, officer, but... the German traitor is gone. It's enough to make a saint swear.'

'Are you sure you locked the door, sir?'

'Of *course* I locked the door. You don't have to be Sherlock Holmes to see the *window* is forced open. She isn't in sight. She must have a five minutes' start.'

'Then we'll begin a search of the village and the fields at once,' the policeman promised. The voices of the two men faded as they hurried out.

Brigit breathed again. She was safe for now. There was a clock on the mantelpiece above the fire, so she would know when it was twelve o'clock. She could climb out from her hiding place and see down the main street of the village to the school, where the bus with her mother on board would stop.

She watched the policeman and the Reverend leave through the front gate and she heard them ordering villagers to start the search for a German spy. Alice followed them out, called from her kitchen to help.

It was over a hundred metres from her escape window to the bus stop beside the school gates. She would never make it without being seen and caught. But the plan she had dreamed up covered that. She would have to work a little faster than she planned, but the house was empty. She knew what she had to do.

Chapter Sixteen

'I've got a blouse and shawl just like that'

Brigit looked quickly through the drawers of the desk and found a cash box full of coins and pound notes. 'There must be a hundred pounds in there,' the girl thought. She took five notes from the bottom of the box. No one would notice they'd gone unless they counted them carefully. By then she hoped she'd be far away. She put the cash box back and said, 'Not only deadly sins but one of the Ten Commandments. The Devil must be really stoking up those fires for me... except I don't believe in you, Mr Devil.'

Brigit took two sheets of writing paper from the desk and scribbled a note on one. She climbed the stairs, hurried past the bedroom she shared with Jean, and climbed more stairs to the small attic room where Alice slept. The room was dark and cold and lit by an oil lamp that the girl turned up to wrap the room in a warm amber glow.

There was a narrow bed, a chest of drawers and a washstand with a jug of cold water. There was no heating in the room. Brigit opened the drawers one at a time till she found a faded black skirt, a blue blouse and a green shawl. When they were laid on the bed she placed the note on the washstand with the pound notes. It read, *'Sorry I had to take your clothes. Please buy some new ones with this money.'*

Another lie.

'Sorry, Alice,' she muttered, and she put the old woman's clothes on over her school uniform. Alice was a small, frail woman and the clothes were a good fit on the girl. Once she was dressed she hurried down the stairs and back to the Reverend's study. The fire wasn't lit because the weather was warm. There were paper and sticks in the hearth ready to light it.

Brigit pushed these to one side and scooped some ashes and soot on to a sheet of the Reverend's writing paper before carrying it carefully back up the stairs to the bathroom.

First, she took the pale wood-ash in the palm of her hand and dabbed it on her face till her skin turned a sickly grey. Then she took a matchstick, dipped it in the soot and drew thin lines that followed the creases on her face to make them look like deep wrinkles. Anyone who looked closely would see the bright young eyes burning in an ashy face. But if she pulled the shawl over her hair and kept her head down she might just get away with it.

Back in the Reverend's study she watched the villagers, led by the constable, searching every house on the main street. Some of the house-owners came out to join the search. Many of them carried walking sticks and pokers, wood axes and kitchen knives. 'They must think I'm a wild animal,' Brigit said with a shake of her head. 'Maybe I am. Nothing's going to stop me from meeting Maman.'

And so she waited. The searchers spread across the fields and found themselves in an argument with a farmer. He seemed to be telling them they were trampling his spring wheat. He carried a shotgun and looked as fierce as the scarecrow that flapped in the centre of the field. Even the constable looked afraid of the gun and backed away with his hands raised to show they meant no harm.

The villagers walked around the outsides of the fields as the angry farmer watched them. Brigit took some biscuits from the pantry and drank water from the kitchen tap. She emptied her suitcase and packed what she needed in a brown-paper carrier bag.

The clock seemed to be creeping round and she began to worry that the Reverend would give up the search and return.

At eleven o'clock the constable called the searchers together and arranged them in a line with about an arm's length between them. The line headed towards the twenty-acre wood with the villagers beating aside the ferns and brambles before they vanished for a long while.

'Just as well I didn't hide there,' Brigit decided.

By half past eleven the search party were back on the main street. One or two brought along dogs to sniff out the fugitive German spy. This time they headed towards the river.

The clock hands came together like praying hands. Twelve. The children were set free from their lessons and Brigit heard their distant screams as they exploded with happiness into the schoolyard. And exactly on time the bus appeared over the top of the valley road and began a smoky, engine-popping roll down towards the village.

Brigit wrapped the shawl over her head, threw her gas mask over her shoulder, picked up her carrier bag and left the Reverend's house behind. 'Poor Jean,' she sighed as she closed the front door for the final time.

She put on her best slow hobble – not too slow or she'd miss the bus – and walked towards the bus stop by the school. There were a few villagers left and they looked at her curiously. Everyone knew everyone who lived here but they'd never seen this strange old woman before. With that carrier bag she must be from a farm in the county, come to Aberpont to shop.

The greengrocer's shop was open and as she passed it, Brigit heard a voice that she knew. 'Well I never. I've got a blouse and shawl just like that.' Alice the cook came to the door of the shop for a closer look. Brigit hobbled faster and reached the bus stop at the same time as the bus. Alice hadn't tried to stop her. No one had stepped in front of her and pulled back the shawl.

But as she began to climb the step into the bus she looked back. Jean Mason was at the railings of the schoolyard. Their eyes met and Jean's mouth fell open. 'Brigit?' she gasped.

Chapter Seventeen

'What are we going to do with you now?'

'Someone said the police were taking you away,' Jean said.

Brigit raised a finger to her lips. 'Shhhh. I have to escape.'

'On a bus?'

'Yes. On a bus. This isn't the movies where the cowboy rides out of town on the fastest pony he can find. Now go away before anyone sees you talking to me.'

'But I'll miss you,' Jean sniffed.

'And I'll miss you too, but if I don't leave now they'll take me away from here anyway. Go.'

Jean nodded and wandered sadly back into the schoolyard where Miss South was organising a game of rounders. Brigit boarded the bus.

'Brigit?' came a voice that startled her.

'Maman!' she cried and saw her mother's baffled face as she walked down the bus to meet her.

'Why are you dressed like that? Is it a school play?'

'I'll explain. Just tell the driver to go.'

Aimee Furst shook her head. 'I only called to see you and say goodbye. You know you can't come with me.'

'I *have* to,' Brigit groaned as she saw the Reverend Williams walking down the high street towards them and Alice shuffling the other way to meet him. The cook's watery eyes were fixed on Brigit's clothes.

Aimee looked and quickly understood her daughter's problem. 'Drive on,' she told the man at the wheel.

'Another passenger? To Pembrokeshire? That'll be two shillings for an old-aged pensioner.' The driver fussed with his ticket machine.

Reverend Williams was a few strides from the bus and calling, 'Driver... we need your help...' while Alice was croaking, 'Stop, thief.'

'*Three* shillings if you set off right now.'

The driver gave a grin and a wink. He crunched the old bus into gear and put his foot on the accelerator. The racing engine gave out clouds of oily smoke that smothered the Reverend Williams. The bus jumped forward like a pouncing cat and Alice had to jump out of the way. She waved a fist as the Reverend broke into a shambling run behind. The constable didn't quite know what was happening but he stepped in front of the bus to find out. The driver blasted his horn and slowed. '*Four* shillings,' Aimee promised, and he gathered speed again as the policeman put his whistle to his lips. The constable took a deep breath of black engine fumes and coughed till his face turned tomato-red.

'I enjoyed that,' the driver said. 'I suppose there'll be trouble for me at the other end.'

'There won't,' Aimee said. She waved a hand at the dozen people on the bus. 'These people are very special. Mr Churchill himself watches over their work. Trust me, no one will dare to ask questions about why we drove out of Aberpont like that.'

The driver nodded, satisfied. 'And what about the old lady that just got on? Is she Churchill's mother?'

Brigit used the shawl to wipe most of the ash and soot off her face. 'It's a young lady... and she's the newest member of Mr Churchill's secret group,' she said.

'Of course you are,' the man said and swung the bus around the rolling, twisting roads of the Cambrian Mountains towards the west. 'We'll be there in four hours. Just in time for tea,' he said.

Aimee sat Brigit down next to her on the bus. 'You can meet all these brave people later. First, I have to know what happened back there in Aberpont. We're a very important group of people and we can't risk our secret getting out.'

'You're not important. You're my maman,' Brigit said with a cheeky grin that made Aimee want to hug her.

'I agree. But it did mean I could get reports from the head of the evacuee department about where you were staying. However, the training I've been doing has been top secret, and who I am isn't widely known. Unfortunately, some unwitting clerk in an office sent out that letter about you to the Reverend Williams before we could stop it. Was that him chasing the bus?'

'It was.'

'Didn't look like a very pleasant person.'

'He's not… I'm going to burn in the fires of Hell several times, he says. But that can't be any worse than what Miss Dennison used to do to us in Castle Bromwich School.'

'I guessed that's why you switched groups and ended up in Aberpont with Hodgehill School. Then I saw you'd been adopted by a priest and thought you'd be safe and happy there.'

Brigit shrugged. 'I was safe but hungry. I think he took us in because it gave him extra ration coupons for more food, and he could eat our share.'

The girl went on to tell her mother the adventures of the morning. 'I told myself I'd make it to the bus… and I did.'

Aimee sighed. 'Yes, but what are we going to do with you now? There's no one to look after you back in Castle Bromwich. Your father will be released next week to work as a doctor in the Spitfire factory, but he'll have to return to the internment camp every evening after work. You can't live with him there.'

'There is someone who will look after me and care for me nearly as well as you would,' Brigit said.

Her mother frowned. 'We have no relations in this country.'

'I didn't say the person was in this country,' the girl replied.

'Then who? Don't tease, Brigit.'

'My grand-maman… your mother.'

Aimee shook her head. 'But… but she's in France. The Germans are about to march in and take over.'

'Yes, I know, but you told me that in the last war your mother's farm was spared because both sides needed the food she produced. I speak perfect French. Grand-maman Colette would love to look after me. And remember what you said in your secret invisible letter?'

Aimee's eyes flew wide with fear. 'Don't let anyone know about that letter. Mr Churchill will shoot me himself if he finds out I told you about our work.'

'Of course I won't tell anyone. But as I *do* know about the letter, I know you'll be working near Bray. If I stay with Grand-maman you may even get to see us from time to time when you're not blowing Germans to the moon.'

The afternoon sun was sinking and shone golden on the Irish Sea as the bus crossed the last range of mountains and began to run down the west coast of Wales. Aimee thought for a long time before she finally said, 'I will talk to Major Ellis when we get to the training camp. Though he won't agree.'

'Don't give in, Maman. Never, never, never give in.'

Her mother smiled. 'You're just like Mr Churchill.'

'Just not so fat and bald,' Brigit said.

Chapter Eighteen

'I could sleep on a rock in the river'

The training camp had been set up quickly. It was simply a square made up of a dozen wooden sheds, nestled in a hidden valley that ran down to the sea. The setting sun shone golden on the water, birds sang in the trees and war seemed impossible in such a peaceful world. It was sheltered by woods and surrounded by a high fence topped with barbed wire. Half a dozen soldiers were on patrol or in lookout towers.

'Is this an SOE camp or a prison?' Brigit asked her mother.

'The fence and the guards are to keep strangers out, not to keep us in,' Aimee said as they stepped down from the bus. The rest of the group followed, a handful of chattering men and women, smiling warmly at Brigit.

'They're all speaking French,' Brigit said.

'Of course,' said Aimee. 'Most of the team are French. We'll be back in France very soon, so we need to get used to the language again… not just speaking French but thinking and dreaming in it. Some of us have been away for a long time.'

The team of saboteurs carried kitbags and were met by an army sergeant and by Major Ellis who said, 'Sergeant Evans here will show you to your huts and tell you the rules – though after training all these months I guess you can quickly settle in anywhere.'

'We've slept in forests and fields, on beaches and mountains. I could sleep on a rock in the river if I had to,' one of the men said.

'We may let you try that, Raoul,' Major Ellis said, and the others laughed. They all seemed relaxed and closer than friends. More like a family. 'I find it hard enough having cold showers,' the major was saying. Everyone shivered at the thought.

Sergeant Evans looked at the major as if he was swallowing vinegar. 'This is a training camp, not a holiday camp… sir.'

'Really? These poor people were told it was a nice little treat for finishing their training.' Everyone chuckled.

'How can they be so happy when they're going to face danger and death?' Brigit asked her maman.

'They're just very brave people,' Aimee said with a shrug.

'Stop talking, you two,' Sergeant Evans barked. 'Yes, you, madam, and the little lady by your side.'

'What?' Brigit asked.

'Major Ellis has told me how you ended up here, miss, but you are under the British army command while you are in this training zone, and you will operate under the rules of the British army. The first rule is you must always obey the commands of a senior officer.'

'A bit like school then,' Brigit said. Aimee gave her a hard nudge to silence her. But it was too late.

Sergeant Evans strode forward and loomed over the girl. He lowered his head and spoke with a voice that sounded like he'd gargled with gravel. 'Not at all like school, madam. At school the punishments are writing a hundred lines or losing your break time. Here we find really nasty jobs for people who disobey – cleaning toilets, sweeping out the huts, peeling potatoes and being locked away for a few days with just bread and water. Do I make myself clear?'

Brigit opened her mouth to reply but Aimee cut in quickly, 'Yes, sir. She understands. Don't you, Brigit?' She nudged her daughter again.

Brigit glared and fixed her lips tight as a rat trap. Sergeant Evans, like the Reverend Williams, would need careful handling. He stepped back as if burned by the girl's stare and went on, 'Sleeping huts here and here, toilet and shower blocks over there. Canteen in the middle and recreation room behind you. Any questions just ask me. Understood?'

'Yes, Sergeant,' came a chorus of voices.

'Training starts tomorrow,' Major Ellis said, 'so get a good night's sleep. Squad dismissed.'

The group of spies and saboteurs didn't look much like an army squad and as they shuffled off to their huts, Sergeant Evans looked at them sourly. Brigit heard him mutter to Major Ellis, 'Give me a week with this lot and I'll have them marching like the Grenadier Guards.'

The major laughed. 'That'll not do them much good in a French field when they're spying out German army secrets. They may not look like your usual soldiers, Sergeant, but they have just as much courage.'

Aimee tugged Brigit along with her to the hut nearest the sea. The walls smelled of fresh wood preserver and the floors of new concrete. A small stove in the corner glowed warm, as the evening air off the Irish Sea sent a chill through the room. Brigit chose the bed next to her maman and unpacked the few things she'd brought in her carrier bag.

Oil lamps were lit as the huts hadn't been fitted with electric. 'Too far from the nearest village,' a tall, dark-haired woman called Yvette explained. But it was cosy and so much more homely than the Reverend Williams' dank bedrooms.

A dreamless sleep soon swallowed Brigit and she woke with the sun to the gentle snoring of women. She dressed quickly and went over to the stove to boil a kettle of water and make a pot of tea. One by one the women rose and moved sleepily across to the stove to enjoy a cup.

Sergeant Evans was waiting on the path between the huts as the sleepy-eyed men drifted out. 'Good morning, ladies, gentlemen… and young lady. In the canteen the cook is preparing a breakfast of bacon, sausage, mushrooms, tomatoes and fried bread.'

Even the sleepiest of the men looked bright-eyed at that. 'Your chiefs have ordered that you have the best food there is. You need to build up your strength. Sadly, you do not get to eat one mouthful until I am satisfied you have earned it.'

Everyone groaned. The sergeant pointed towards the sea. The gate to the beach is open. Everyone will take a cup and fill it with seawater. The first one back gets extra bacon and egg. Is that clear?'

'So it's a race,' Brigit said.

'Well done. I can see there are no flies on you, your ladyship. You can't even see where they rested. Yes, it's a race.'

'Not a fair race, though. I mean, in the Olympics the men and women run separately because the men are faster and sure to win.'

The sergeant looked up at the sky. 'Very well. The first man *and* the first woman to bring back a cup of seawater will be rewarded with extra breakfast. Is *that* fair?'

Brigit shook her head. 'And the first runner under the age of sixteen… to make it really fair.'

Sergeant Evans gave her his fiercest glare. 'Do I look stupid?'

'Well…' Brigit began.

'She will run with the other women,' Aimee said quickly.

Everyone picked up a cup and before the sergeant had a chance to say 'go' some set off at a sprint down the path.

And still the war felt a million miles away.

Chapter Nineteen

'The Battle of Britain is about to begin'

June–September 1940: Pembrokeshire, West Wales

Every morning in the training camp was the same. A run followed by a cold shower followed by a fine breakfast that would have satisfied even the Reverend Williams.

The days passed in warm rain and sunshine. At first Brigit was treated like a child, patted on the head and told she was doing well... even when she knew she wasn't. But she quickly proved herself as clever and fit as the adults and soon everyone except the sergeant began to treat her as an equal.

In the evenings they sat in the recreation room listening to the news of the war on the crackling radio powered by a generator. All the happiness of the day seemed to slip away as the news was always bad. The British army had landed in France. But by early June they had been driven back to the sea. The radio said in gloomy tones:

'The British commander-in-chief, General Gort, has been forced to retreat to the French coast at Dunkirk. The troops are waiting, under merciless fire, to be rescued from the beaches. A call has gone out to all owners of seaworthy vessels to travel to Dunkirk to take the troops off the beaches.'

Large ships and tiny pleasure boats set off. More than 300,000 men were rescued, among them some 140,000 French who were desperate to form a Free French army that would return and free their homeland one day. But first they needed the saboteurs to make that return easier.

'When do we go?' Raoul asked.

'You have learned many skills at your camps all over Britain,' Major Ellis said. 'You are very good. This is the place where you will become perfect. The difference between good and perfect may be the difference between life and death. Your life. Your death.'

Major Ellis was busy with workmen building an assault course. Climbing nets and tunnels, obstacles and balance beams, rope swings and mud ditches. 'We need you to be strong and fit for anything,' the major told the group. The saboteurs set off. Half dropped out, beaten before they reached the end. The finishers were timed. Brigit was nimble and light. Her time was the fastest.

Sergeant Evans gave the results. He looked at Brigit with a new respect.

The work took place in the training hut and Brigit joined in. Major Ellis had said she could attend a village school about a ten-mile bus journey to the east. But Aimee pointed out that it would soon be the summer holidays and not worth it. So Brigit joined the training classes.

In a few hours she had learned to take apart a German pistol and put it back together. 'Why not a British pistol, Maman?' she asked.

'If the German secret police – the Gestapo – find us with a German pistol we can tell them we found it where some careless German soldier had left it. They may punish us with a few weeks in prison. But if they find us with a *British* weapon they'll know we are spies. They will shoot us.'

It sounded so dangerous Brigit decided then that she couldn't let her maman go to France alone.

Bad news followed bad news. Later in June, Italy joined the war on the side of Germany. Before the end of the month, France had surrendered and the Germans took over.

The French leader Marshal Pétain told his people: '*It is with broken heart that I tell you today that fighting must cease.*'

Winston Churchill told the British: '*The news from France is very bad, and I grieve for the gallant French people.*' The saboteurs in the camp held back their tears as Churchill finished: *'We are sure that in the end all will be well.'*

Mr Churchill stayed strong and told his people what they had already guessed: *'The Battle of France is over. I expect that the Battle of Britain is about to begin. The whole fury and might of the enemy must very soon be turned on us. Hitler knows that he will have to break us in this island or lose the war. If we can stand up to him, all Europe may be free, and the life of the world may move forward into broad, sunlit uplands. But if we fail, then the whole world will sink into the abyss of a new Dark Age. Let us therefore brace ourselves to our duties, and so bear ourselves that if the British Empire and its Commonwealth last for a thousand years, men will still say, "This was their finest hour".'*

'The Battle of Britain,' Yvette said. 'We may not even get to France. Germany could come to us.'

'We'll be ready,' Brigit said, most fierce of all. Just three weeks ago the SOE agents would have smiled and patted her on the head. But now they nodded for they knew she was right.

The next day they trained more fiercely than ever before. Everyone finished the assault course.

And Winston Churchill was right about the Battle of Britain but it began in the air, not on the landing-beaches.

In July reports came of waves of German bombers attacking the east of Britain. In September the bombers stopped attacking airfields and turned their weapons on the defenceless people in the towns. The Blitz that had smashed Poland and Belgium was raining down on London.

'The Castle Bromwich Spitfires will blow the bombers apart,' Brigit said. The saboteurs prayed that she would be right.

Still they trained. From the Welsh beach they learned to operate miniature submarines, but Aimee took a different course. She learned to fly small aircraft. When she had passed her final test, she was able to take her daughter up and over West Wales. The fields of gold and green and brown with silver roads and blue rivers spread out below like a quilt.

And when they landed and returned to camp it was to an excited group of French friends. 'We must be leaving for France soon. We've been ordered to scrub the huts till they are spotless. We must be moving out.'

Raoul shouted across to Sergeant Evans, 'Is that right, Sergeant? Are we off to France?'

'If I knew that I would not be allowed to tell you,' the sergeant replied gruffly.

'So why are we doing all this cleaning?' Yvette sighed.

'Because tomorrow we've been promised a very important visitor.'

'Must be the king,' Brigit guessed.

She was wrong.

Chapter Twenty

'Let me show you how it's done...'

No one slept much that night. Yvette said, 'If we have an important visitor then it's because we are about to be sent to France. They have come to say goodbye.'

The other women in the sleeping hut nodded.

The next morning they ran to the sea and back, showered and trained. Sergeant Evans said, 'Our visitor will be arriving at 1300 hours. We need to entertain them. Now, for the next hour, we'll break into groups. We will plan demonstrations. Yvette, you can show how you would kill a man... Raoul can be the victim.'

'Thanks,' Raoul muttered.

'Make it look real. We will have one man and one woman on the assault course – and there will be a prize for the first to finish. Two of you will put a pistol together and then race to the target range to fire six shots into one of the dummies. A bar of chocolate for the winner. Someone can plant a real pencil bomb to show how powerful they are.'

'Maybe we could blow up your office?' Aimee said with a grin.

The sergeant narrowed his eyes and said, 'Or maybe we could use you as one of the targets, Mrs Furst? A live target. Very good practice.'

'My comrades would refuse to shoot me,' Aimee said and looked around at her friends.

'For a bar of chocolate?' Yvette said. 'Oh, but I think we would shoot our own mothers, isn't that right, ladies?' They all agreed they would.

Aimee stuck out her tongue at them.

'I want someone to land by parachute – Aimee, you can fly the light aircraft and drop Jacques. Then land on the beach. Our important visitor will be pleased to see a woman pilot. And finally I need someone to use camouflage to go through the woods and get past the guards without being seen.'

'I'll do that,' Brigit offered.

Sergeant Evans pulled a face. 'I'm afraid I can't allow that. You are not an SOE member. In fact, it would be better if you weren't here at all. How do we explain a girl in the training camp? We will send you to the nearest village to have a nice lunch.'

'I have done all the training,' Brigit said fiercely. 'There's no reason why I can't go to France. I can live with my grand-maman and help Maman when she needs it.'

'We've talked about this and you know it can't happen.' Aimee sighed. 'Isn't that right, Sergeant Evans?'

'SOE plans are for Major Ellis to decide. My job is just to train you. But, if you did ask me, I'd say it was ridiculous.'

'Just as well I'm not asking you,' Brigit muttered under her breath. Aloud, she said, 'We'll see.'

The saboteurs hurried off to practise their demonstrations while Brigit wandered around and helped where she could. At noon one of the guards brought the Humber FWD camp car to the front gate and Sergeant Evans opened the door for Brigit to step inside. She smiled sweetly at him and clutched her brown-paper carrier bag close. 'I hope you have a nice afternoon with the king,' she said. 'I could have offered to polish his crown for him.'

'It might not be the king,' the sergeant said.

'You would say that,' Brigit thought.

'I'll send the car to collect you at 1400 hours when the visitor has gone,' the sergeant went on. 'Here is some money and a few ration coupons. I'll see you around 1415,' he said and slammed the door.

'That's what you think,' Brigit said quietly.

The driver was one of the silent guards and that suited Brigit. He crunched through the gears and raced the engine till the inside smelled of oil and smoke. Brigit sat in the back seat and was able to make her plans while watching carefully which turnings they took. She guessed they travelled three miles before they reached a village with some Welsh name she couldn't say.

They pulled up outside a tea shop where men and women in shorts and cycling gear mixed with others with backpacks and boots. 'Cyclists and walkers welcome,' a sign said.

The driver got out and opened the door for Brigit. He spoke for the first time. 'I'll be back at 1400 hours,' he said. 'That'll be nice for you. You can have a cream cake or a scone and a cup of tea.'

Brigit walked up the path to the front of the café, which was crowded with chattering people mostly too old to serve in the war. As she reached the door she heard the gears of the Humber crunch and the heavy vehicle rolled away in a cloud of smoke and petrol fumes.

She turned around and walked back to the low white fence at the edge of the road where bicycles were propped. For a moment she thought about taking one of the bikes. 'You took Alice's clothes,' she said to herself. 'You can steal a bike. Yes, Brigit Furst, a real Robin Hood… stealing from the old to help poor Brigit.'

She took a deep breath and left the bicycles behind. 'Anyway, there were racing bikes there – if anyone saw me go they'd race after me and catch me in a quarter of a mile.'

As she left the village behind, the clock on the church tower struck twelve. 'I can just about make it,' she guessed.

The road back to the training camp was rough and stony. She guessed not many cyclists would head this way or their tyres would puncture. 'They'll puncture my feet if these thin shoes give way,' she sighed.

Brigit tried to walk on the grass at the side of the road but some of the sharp stones had rolled into the grass and were hidden there. That made it worse. The autumn weather was warm, and Brigit's face was red.

'Blood, toil, tears and sweat,' she chanted as she marched along. She stopped for a moment. 'No tears,' she decided. 'Blood, toil and sweat. That's what'll get me there.'

She heard a car crunching carefully down the road behind her. She ran up the grass bank, pushed through the hedge at the top and threw herself to the ground. She raised her head enough to see a large black Rolls-Royce glide past her, but not enough to see who the famous visitor was. 'It has to be King

George,' she said as the car disappeared round the bend and on the last stretch to the camp gates.

Brigit slid back down the grass to the road. 'What did you want, Sergeant Evans? Remind me? Ah, yes. Someone to use camouflage to go through the woods and get past the guards without being seen? Let me show you how it's done...'

Chapter Twenty-One

'Hello, King George. Pleased to meet you'

When Brigit had walked round the bend in the road she saw the Rolls-Royce being driven through the main gate. The guard closed it and Sergeant Evans would make sure she was kept outside until their important guest had left. And then it could be a week of bread and water.

She stepped off the road once again and into the wood that shielded the right side of the camp. The old trees were still and cool in the afternoon heat. The green light was restful on her eyes. Squirrels and voles, a fox and a deer ran away from her as she crept alongside the camp fence till she came to the first watchtower. The soldier on guard was looking towards the camp instead of into the woods to seek out spies and assassins. He was looking at the famous visitor.

Brigit stepped behind a wide oak and opened her carrier bag. She pulled out the clothes she'd stolen from Alice the cook. After she had pulled the shawl over her hair it covered most of her face.

She had learned enough Welsh back in Aberpont to say a few sentences and knew the soldiers were English. *'Esgusodwch fi, dyn ifanc,'* she croaked in a voice that could have come from the witch in *Hansel and Gretel*.

The soldier jumped away from the rail, slid a bullet into the chamber of his rifle and pointed it shakily towards the oak tree. 'Who's there?'

'Ydych chi'n siarad Cymraeg?' she asked.

'Speak English, you German joker,' he called.

'Sorry. I'm *Welsh*, not *German*,' Brigit said in English but with an accent she'd borrowed from the Reverend Williams.

As the man's eyes grew used to the shadows of the woods he could make out an old woman in a shawl. 'What do you want, you old Welsh witch?'

'I just wanted to ask you a *question*.'

'I'm busy.'

'I just wanted to ask if you *knew* about the man who landed in our *fields* – we have the farm on the other side of these woods.'

'Landed?'

'In one of those… *parasiwt* things.'

'*Parasiwt*? You mean parachute?'

'That's what I said. He jumped out of a plane with black *crosses* on the wings. He left the *parasiwt* in the field and headed this way with a *rifle*.'

'A German paratrooper?' the man cried. 'I can't see one.'

'You wouldn't. He's at the corner where the woods meet the seashore. You can't see it from *this* watchtower and you can't quite see it from the tower that looks towards the *sea*. It's in what you'd call a *blind* spot.'

'But we have an important visitor,' the guard wailed and began to leap down the wooden ladder to the tower, two steps at a time.

'Don't bother to say thanks to a helpful old farmer's wife,' Brigit sighed. She threw off her disguise and ran to the foot of the tower. Using all the strength and skill she'd learned from the assault course she began to climb upwards, using the wooden cross-braces on the tower like rungs of a ladder. She reached the height of the barbed wire on top of the fence, threw her leg over and placed her hands between the sharp spikes on the wire. She hung for a moment and dropped to the ground.

'You thought you'd keep me away from meeting the king, did you, Sergeant Evans?' she said as she ran over to the shower hut and pushed herself flat against the back. Her plan was to stroll out and say, 'Hello, King George. Pleased to meet you. I was hoping you'd help me to get to France.'

But the plan hadn't worked. As soon as the guard had climbed down he ran towards the huts shouting, 'German paratrooper landed. Far corner of the camp where the wood meets the seashore.'

Major Ellis grabbed the guest, a heavy man in army battledress and dragged him inside the nearest hut – the men's sleeping quarters. Sergeant Evans gathered the other guards while the saboteurs went into the weapons' store and came out with the pistols they trained with on the firing range.

There was no time to form in battle order. Everyone with a weapon, guards or SOE members, ran towards the north-west corner of the camp.

'Oooops,' Brigit said when she saw the storm of anger she'd created. She knew she'd have to bury the old farmer's wife in the woods – or her clothes at any rate – as soon as she could get outside again. 'If they ever find out, I'll not be on bread and water for a week. It'll be for the rest of my life.'

She stepped out from her hiding place behind the shower hut and gazed at the men's sleeping hut. That was where she'd seen Major Ellis take the important visitor. She wanted to speak to the king and beg him to let her go to France, but she knew the sergeant and the other SOE members would hush her and pull her away. 'But it's better this way,' she said and rubbed her hands. 'This way I get to see him alone – or at least just with Major Ellis, and he understands.'

Overhead a small aeroplane buzzed and circled the camp and headed towards the beach to land. Aimee Furst, the pilot, looked down and wondered what was going on. She was dead on time, but no one was waiting to watch her land, the way they'd planned. Everyone was crowding towards a corner of the field and guns glinted in the sun. She lifted the nose of the plane and decided to make another circle around the hills to the east before coming back.

Brigit gave a tiny wave to the plane as it disappeared, took a deep breath and strode over to the hut where the important visitor was sheltering. She knocked politely on the door. After a moment Major Ellis opened it and pointed a pistol in her face. 'Brigit? I thought you were in the village?'

'I wanted a word with the king,' she said.

Major Ellis looked more annoyed than she'd ever seen him. He threw open the door and let Brigit enter the hut. 'No king,' he said.

Brigit looked at the important visitor, sitting on a bed.

'Oh. It's *you*,' she gasped.

Chapter Twenty-Two

'I must go and meet with danger'

'Come in and sit down,' the important guest said. Brigit felt a little weak at the knees but managed to walk across to one of the beds and sit opposite the great man. Her mouth was dry, but she managed to say, 'You're Winston Churchill, aren't you?'

The man put on a serious face and leaned towards her. 'There is a German paratrooper in this camp, probably here to assassinate me. It's not you, is it?'

Brigit laughed and relaxed a little. 'It's just a story some crazy old farmer's wife told a guard. You are safe, Mr Churchill.'

The prime minister took a handkerchief from the pocket of his battledress jacket and wiped the sweat off his brow. 'I'm pleased to hear it. What is a young lady like you doing here?'

'I'm Brigit, and my maman is training with the SOE.'

'So you are not an enemy come to assassinate me. I am pleased. Mind you, I am not afraid to face the enemy guns, you know? I rode with the cavalry at the Battle of Omdurman in the Sudan in 1898.'

'I know you fought in the Boer War, Mr Churchill.'

The man chuckled. 'What an adventure that was. People think prime ministers are dull fellows, but I have seen dangers and escapes.' He turned to Major Ellis. 'Light me a cigar, there's a good chap, and I'll tell our young guest the tale.'

Churchill said he had been a newspaper reporter in the war in South Africa. He marched with the British army. But when they were defeated, the

South Africans (the Boers) captured him and shut him in a camp as a prisoner of war.

'They locked me away in an old school. Imagine that? A school used as a prison.'

Brigit nodded. 'A bit like my school back in Castle Bromwich.'

'I timed the guard patrols. I spotted a few minutes every hour when no one was watching the ten-foot wall that surrounded the camp. A blind spot.'

Brigit grinned. 'That's what I told the guard on this camp,' she said.

'When?' Major Ellis asked sharply.

The girl blushed. 'I mean that's what the old farmer's wife told the guard. He left his watchtower and I climbed in. But it wasn't me. I didn't trick the guard. It was the old woman. Ask the guard.'

The major looked at her sternly. 'I will be asking him a lot of questions when all this fuss has died down.'

'So you escaped, Mr Churchill?' Brigit said quickly.

Churchill sucked on his cigar and watched the smoke drift up to the roof. 'It was 12 December 1899. I waited for the moment to happen and then raced forward and scaled the wall. But my troubles were just starting. I had to make a three hundred-mile journey to East Africa. I only had seventy-five pounds and some chocolate to eat.'

'You couldn't walk three hundred miles,' Brigit said.

'No. I went to the rail yards and jumped on a freight train. I found a wagon with empty coal sacks. Very comfy.' He gave a sudden laugh. 'That was when I found I was sharing the space with a vulture. It looked very interested in me.'

'But you escaped?'

'I had to get off the train because I was so hungry and thirsty. I tried knocking on the door of a strange house. And, as luck would have it, that was the house of the only Englishman for miles around. The Boers were offering a reward of twenty-five pounds for my capture... dead or alive. But that Englishman hid me down a mine shaft... plenty of food and cigars to keep me going and I read books by the light of a candle.'

'I did that in Aberpont when I was evacuated,' Brigit said.

'You hid down a mine?'

'No. I read a book by candlelight.'

'Ah. Anyway, they hid me on a train carrying wool to East Africa and it took me to freedom. I went back to South Africa to fight the Boers. This time we won, and I had the pleasure of riding into their prison camp and telling the British prisoners they were free.'

'That's an amazing story,' Brigit said.

Churchill looked out of the window at the fences beyond the huts. 'I never feel *comfortable* in a place like this. Being fenced in sends a shiver down to my boots.'

'So why did you come here, sir?' Major Ellis asked.

The prime minister rose to his feet. 'When I was in school we read plays by William Shakespeare. Have you ever read Shakespeare, Brigit?'

'No, Mr Churchill. We didn't read plays or stories or poems. We just did practice tests, so we could pass the exams at the end of every term.'

'Oh dear. I'll have to change that when this war is over. I didn't always like Shakespeare at school. It's in later years I saw how wise he was. I always remember he said something about the perils of this world. He said you shouldn't sit back and wait for menaces to come and find you. What you should be doing is going out to meet them head-on. Do you remember Shakespeare's words, Major Ellis?'

'I must go and meet with danger there, or it will seek me in another place,' the major said. 'From the play *Henry IV, Part 2*.'

'That's it.' Churchill nodded. 'Let's not wait for Mr Hitler to attack us. Let's go and attack him in any way we can.'

'That's what Maman and the SOE are going to do,' Brigit said.

'Exactly. I formed the SOE to wreck the German plans – to hold them up just long enough for us to build our strength and go on the attack. The Royal Air Force is doing it now. The army won't be far behind. That's why I'm here. I cannot let my SOE agents go to war without seeing them for myself and finding out a little about each one. I am the one sending them to meet with danger. If anything goes wrong, it will be me to blame.'

The girl thought for a while. 'But when my maman goes to… meet with danger… she will need help.'

'The SOE will get all the help I can give them,' Churchill promised.

'Yes, but she may need someone in France. Someone like me.'

Chapter Twenty-Three

'Mr Churchill is a fool'

Winston Churchill looked at Brigit and his face was serious. 'That is the sort of spirit that will win the war for us,' he said. 'I wish I could allow you to go, but…'

'But you are going to say I am too young.' Brigit sighed. 'Maman was my age in the last war. And she saved hundreds of lives.'

Churchill frowned. 'Did she? And she is here now?' He looked up at Major Ellis.

The major nodded. 'Yes, sir. Her name was Aimee Fletcher and she lived at Bray-on-Somme.

We suspected a spy – Silver Hand we called him – and it was Aimee who found the way to put a stop to him. Aimee's mother still lives in Bray. That's where we'll drop her.'

'And that Aimee Fletcher has grown up to be an SOE agent?'

'Yes, sir. When you set up the SOE she was top of our list. At the end of the Great War she helped to get a young German soldier home. He came back to France after the war and married Aimee. She is Aimee Furst now.'

'I remember now,' Churchill said. 'I heard the story of Silver Hand many years ago, but I used to think it was a legend. How remarkable. Aimee was a brave girl.' He looked across at Brigit. 'And she has a brave daughter.'

'Maman was my age when she took all those risks. If *she* could help the British in the last war, then she can't object to *me* helping them in this war. And anyway, I don't have anywhere else to go.'

'Your father? The German soldier?' Churchill asked.

'He's in an internment camp back in Castle Bromwich,' Major Ellis said. 'He's a doctor and helps in the Spitfire factory, but he has to return to the internment camp every night.'

'Let him go back to the family home,' Churchill growled.

'We tried, sir, but the Castle Bromwich people didn't like the idea of a German living in their street. They threw bricks through his windows. Every time we repaired them they were smashed again. He is safer in the camp.'

'Then Brigit here may be safer with her grand-maman in Bray,' the prime minister said.

'Brigit has learned a lot of SOE skills, but she can't land on a parachute.'

'Major Ellis, we have the wonderful Westland Lysander aeroplane that can land on a field the size of a playing card. Brigit and her mother can squeeze into the passenger seat and we shall drop them by the side of the Somme. There must be a good field near there?'

The major smiled. 'There is the airfield the famous German fighter pilot, the Red Baron, used in the Great War.'

'Then it is decided,' Churchill said and sucked on his cigar till it glowed like a coke oven.

There was a knock at the door and it opened. Sergeant Evans entered and saluted. 'All clear, sir. False alarm. It seems some old farmer's wife was stirring up trouble – they don't all like us moving on to their land.'

'Very good, Sergeant,' Major Ellis said. 'We will carry on with the displays. Firing range next isn't it?'

'Yes, sir. Excuse me, sir, but would you like some of us to search outside the fence and see if we can find any clues about the old woman who said we were under attack?'

Brigit held her breath. She had covered Alice's shawl and skirt with a few dead leaves, but they would soon be found. All the SOE agents had seen her get on to the bus at Aberpont when she was wearing those clothes. It would be a year on bread and water.

Major Ellis was looking at the girl with sharp eyes and the ghost of a smile. He spoke slowly. 'No, Sergeant, everyone is too busy. But Brigit here can do a search in the woods near the north watchtower. I'm not sure what you're doing back here, but you may as well make yourself useful. You don't mind, do you, Brigit?'

Brigit started breathing again and babbled, 'No, Major… glad to, Major…'

'And if you find any clues you know what to do with them?'

Brigit nodded and tried to look serious. 'I know exactly what to do with them,' she said.

'Then Mr Churchill can enjoy the rest of the displays we have.'

Churchill nodded to Brigit. 'I hope to see you before I go,' he said, then he dusted cigar ash off his battledress and followed Sergeant Evans out of the door.

*

It was almost two o'clock when the SOE agents assembled again by the huts. Brigit was back in time to join them as they lined up.

Aimee Furst had made a perfect landing on the beach and the prime minister met her and shook her warmly by the hand as she arrived from the beach gate. He then took her aside and spoke quietly, so no one could hear them. Aimee looked up and met Brigit's eyes. She was frowning and shaking her head. Mr Churchill hit the palm of his hand with his fist, determined. Aimee's shoulders sagged, defeated, and she nodded slowly. She walked across to join her daughter at the end of the line of agents.

'It seems you will be seeing Grand-maman in France after all,' she whispered.

'Mr Churchill ordered it,' Brigit said.

'Mr Churchill is a fool,' her maman said crossly.

The prime minister stood in front of the group and said farewell. 'I envy you,' he said. 'I am sitting in an air-raid shelter in London, giving orders. But you are going out there and *doing* something. We don't know when you may be needed. We do know you will be ready to meet with danger when the time comes. Farewell, I wish you luck and I hope to see you all back safe when we have won this war.' He strode across to the waiting car and disappeared.

'A great man,' Yvette said.

'A fool,' Aimee Furst snapped.

Part II

Chapter Twenty-Four

'They're looking for the agents'

Monday, 2 June 1941:
Bray-on-Somme, France

'We do know you will be ready when the time comes,' Mr Churchill had said. The group continued their daily training until they were close to perfect in all the skills they'd need. And suddenly that time *had* come. One bright June morning, Brigit and Aimee found out they would be flying to France that evening.

The aeroplane was a Lysander – the airmen called them 'Lizzies'. This one was painted black to hide it from the German planes as it flew eastwards over France. A half-moon helped the pilot follow the silver line of the River Somme.

It was cramped and noisy. It was meant for a pilot and one passenger, but Brigit and Aimee Furst were squeezed into it with their equipment in suitcases; a radio, weapons and bombs, French money and spare clothes, identity papers (fake of course) and maps disguised to look like playing cards.

It was too noisy for Aimee and her daughter to talk. The woman looked at the river below and tapped the pilot on the shoulder. 'That's Amiens,' she shouted over the noise of the Bristol Mercury engine.

He nodded and slowed the engine till the small plane lost height and dropped to just two metres above the river. 'Bray.' Aimee pointed to the left. 'The landing field is half a mile ahead.'

All three peered into the deep grey of the moonlit fields and the inky blackness of the tree shadows by the edge of the river. 'There,' Brigit cried, excited that she'd been the first to spot the flash of a torch.

The pilot climbed a few metres and turned the Lizzie to face west. This time the French saboteurs on the ground showed four torches. They made the corners of an oblong of smooth grass where the plane could land safely. The pilot lowered the speed till the plane dropped on to the field and he cut back on the engine so it rolled to a stop in less than two hundred metres.

This was the risky time. Aimee threw open the door as the French agents ran to the plane and Brigit passed the precious equipment to them silently. There was a small ladder below the plane's side door and Brigit scrambled down it, followed by her mother.

The French helpers looked nervous. If a German patrol went past now there would be no escape. No excuses of 'Sorry, officer, I was just walking down the Bray road at midnight and I saw this plane land'.

The two women ran to the east end of the field and lit their torches so the pilot could see how far he could go before he ran into the hedge at the end of the field. The two men carried the cases and hurried Aimee and Brigit to the gate on to the road.

The engine on the Lysander raced and the plane began to speed towards the torches. It was another time of great risk as the engine noise could be heard in Bray. The plane lifted into the starry sky and in the light of the moon Brigit was sure the pilot waggled its wings in a farewell wave. It had all taken less than three minutes.

The torches were turned off and the women hurried across the field to join the others. They didn't need lights as they knew these paths across the fields well. Staying on the roads would have been easier but a German army patrol car could have come along so quickly they'd have had no time to get through a gateway in a field to hide. They'd be trapped like a hare in the lantern light of a poacher. And their end would have been the same. Shot dead.

When they were clear of the road they spoke for the first time. The tall, elderly woman wrapped an arm round the girl's shoulder. 'Hello, Brigit. You've grown since I last saw you.'

'Hello, Grand-maman,' she said.

'I still say it's wrong to bring a child,' the larger of the men grumbled. His worn clothes were stretched over his body that had the muscles of an ox.

'This is Charles Legrande – but everyone calls him Blacksmith Legrande.'

'You weren't here in the last war,' the other French woman said. 'Aimee was a child then, but she did as much as anyone to help us win, isn't that right, Aimee?'

'Thank you,' Aimee said as they reached a stile in the fence between two fields and climbed over. 'You must be Madame Marie Marcel... the teacher.'

'I am... and the other joker in our pack is Henri Caron, a newspaper reporter.'

'I remember Henri,' Aimee said. 'We were at Bray School together. Good to see you again, Henri.'

'And you,' the small man said. 'Come back to save France – again,' he said, and Brigit thought she heard a slight sneer in his voice. Aimee must have heard it too because she replied, 'No, I'm just here to help the brave French people save themselves. Brave French people like you, Henri.'

'And me,' Blacksmith Legrande said as he puffed and wheezed up the slope of the fields that climbed from the river.

Then he stopped. And the rest of the Resistance workers froze as they heard the sound of a motorcycle whine down the road from Bray, followed by the louder rumble of a troop lorry trying to keep up with it.

'The army. They heard the Lysander take off and they're looking for the agents that landed.'

'They are too slow then,' Henri Caron said with a sniff.

'They might start checking houses, to see who's missing from their beds. We'd better get home as quickly as we can,' Madame Marcel said. 'Let's meet at Colette's farmhouse tomorrow, an hour after dark.'

Her schoolteacher voice got no argument from the others, who hurried off in the shadows of the hedgerows to the safety of their own homes. 'Come along,' Colette Fletcher said. 'Our farmhouse is just at the end of this track.' She picked up one of the cases and led the way.

The excitement of the flight and the race from the airfield had kept Brigit awake. Now she suddenly felt tired to the marrow of her bones. She followed her grandmother and mother up the dusty track, desperate for a warm bed and a long sleep.

Berlin, Germany

General Fischer stretched his weary legs. A Gestapo officer in a black uniform stood at the other side of his desk. 'Time for my bed, Colonel Roth.'

'Just one more report, sir,' the thin-faced Roth replied.

'Can it wait until tomorrow?'

'No, sir.'

'Have we won the war yet?'

'No, sir.'

'Then it can wait until tomorrow. Goodnight, Colonel.'

The general rose to his feet and wandered out of his room to find the best restaurant in Berlin.

Chapter Twenty-Five

'We aren't fools, but we need help'

Tuesday, 3 June 1941: Bray-on-Somme

The first meeting of the Bray Resistance group was as cold and wild as a winter storm from the Ural Mountains.

Colette had a table laid with home-baked bread along with golden butter and cheese made from the milk of her own cows. Brigit drank milk while Blacksmith Legrande supped wine from a half-litre tankard. Henri Caron, the reporter, arrived next: his narrow pointed nose seemed to sniff the farmhouse air with a little disgust. He picked at a little bread and cheese as if it were poisoned rat bait.

But when schoolteacher Marie Marcel arrived, the storm turned to thunder. She ignored the food on the table and sat heavily on the bench. 'So, Aimee Fletcher...' she began.

'Aimee Furst,' Brigit's mother said.

'Ah yes, I am forgetting you married one of the *enemy*.'

Aimee nodded wearily. 'One of the enemy who came back here after the war to be a doctor.'

'Then the people of Bray refused to go to his surgery. They spat at him on the street and drove you to Britain,' Henri Caron said with a touch of joyful spite in his whining voice. Brigit decided she didn't like the little reporter.

'I understand what you are saying,' Aimee said calmly. 'But he hates the new Germany – Hitler's Germany – as much as we do.'

'I doubt it,' Marie Marcel snorted.

'But that's not the point,' Henri Caron put in. 'The point is, we asked the British Secret Service for weapons to fight the Germans. And what did they send us?'

'A woman and a child,' Blacksmith Legrande said with a slow nod of his brown-bear head.

Brigit could see the anger in her mother's eyes. 'No. A *trained* agent and a helper that no Gestapo officer would ever suspect,' Aimee replied.

'We don't need a trained agent,' the schoolteacher hissed. 'Henri Caron goes around asking questions – he is a reporter, so no one can guess he is gathering secrets. I am a teacher and I do the planning as carefully as one of my lesson plans. Blacksmith Legrande here has the muscle. Last week he dragged a huge tree trunk on to the railway line to Amiens and stopped the German troop trains for six hours.'

Aimee closed her eyes and tried to keep her temper. 'But if you'd blown up a locomotive – or a stretch of track – you'd have done much more damage,' she said.

Marie Marcel slapped a hand on the table. 'Exactly. That's why we need bombs and weapons, not agents and their brat children.'

Before Brigit could answer, Aimee said quietly, 'Then the first victims of the bombs would be you.

You aren't trained to use them. I need to show you how they work, or you will kill yourself or innocent French people.'

'We aren't fools,' Henri Caron said.

'No. We aren't fools, but we need help,' Brigit's grand-maman put in.

'I need no help to spy on German troops,' the reporter insisted. 'I have vital information that will help the British bombers target the railheads and the troop camps, the weapon factories and the launch pads for the new rockets they are making. Rockets that can't be stopped when they start raining down on London. Vital information.'

'Useless information,' Brigit said.

The adults turned to look at her. Marie Marcel's eyes burned with anger. 'How dare you!' Henri Caron raged.

'Let me explain,' Brigit said. 'You have all of this information. But it is only precious when it is in the hands of the British. Now, let me tell you what will happen when you try to send it. The Germans have radio detectors working all the time. They will track down your radio. Where do you send your messages from?'

'My office, of course,' Henri said with a shrug.

'So they track you down to your office and shoot you,' Brigit explained.

'Only after they've tortured him to betray Marie and Blacksmith Legrande, your grand-maman, you and me,' Aimee reminded her. She looked at Henri. 'To be safe you need to send messages – in our SOE codes – from the open. You send the message quickly so the Germans can't track it. Then you move away in case they did get a bearing on your hiding place.'

'I did it before,' Henri sniffed. 'I sent the message asking for help from the SOE.'

'Yes, I talked to the radio people in Britain. It wasn't in code and the experts said it took you nearly ten minutes to send a simple message.'

'The Germans didn't track him,' Blacksmith Legrande said with a frown that wrinkled his wide, low forehead.

'He was lucky. They weren't expecting to find saboteurs in Bray, so they weren't checking for radio calls then. That tree on the line will change all that. Their trackers are getting better all the time. If Henri tries to send a ten-minute radio message again they will catch him,' Aimee explained.

'So how do we send messages safely?' Colette asked.

'With a trained operator – I am quick, but Brigit is like lightning. At a set time every week, but from a different place – a wood to the east one week, a field to the west the next.'

Henri Caron showed a pained face. 'And how do you get electric to the middle of a wood?' he asked and sat back, happy that he had defeated Aimee.

'Our radios work off batteries. They are small enough to carry in a suitcase and powerful enough for the messages to reach England.'

'Oh,' the little reporter said, and the smugness slid from his face.

Colette leaned forward. 'The British need us,' she said. 'But we need the help of people like Aimee and Brigit.'

'You would say that. They're your family,' Marie Marcel put in bitterly.

Brigit threw up her hands. 'We're all here to fight the Germans. But here we are, fighting each other. You're supposed to be grown-ups. So, grow up.'

There was a shamed silence in the farmhouse kitchen. So quiet they could hear the marching of boots up to the front door. They looked fearful. Then came the heavy knock and the voice shouting, 'Anyone at home?' The man spoke in French. French with a strong German accent.

Chapter Twenty-Six

'I'm afraid to open the door in the dark'

The French saboteurs rose to their feet in panic. 'Quickly,' Colette hissed. 'Into the attic.'

'No, Maman,' Aimee moaned. 'There is no way out from there.'

'If they search the house, you'll be trapped,' Brigit said, remembering the lessons the SOE agents had been taught in the camp.

'We were trained to hide in a place with another way out,' her mother said. 'Go out of the back door and into the barn. Brigit, you stay here. Marie, Charles and Henri, follow me.'

They hurried across the stone floor as quietly as their boots would allow, while Colette went to the door. She looked back and her eyes went wide in horror. There were six cups and plates on the table. 'Get rid of four,' she whispered to Brigit who understood at once.

Colette turned back to the door that was being hammered on again. 'Who's there?' she demanded.

'Corporal Rudolf Muller of the Gestapo,' came the reply.

Brigit was still racing round the table and putting the dirty plates in the sink, rinsing them and drying them. She would need another minute.

'I'm an old lady... alone here except for my young granddaughter. Can't you come back in the daylight? I'm afraid to open the door in the dark.'

'I don't mean you any harm,' Corporal Rudolf said.

'You're the Gestapo.'

'Not tonight,' he replied.

'But you said you were,' Colette reminded him. Brigit was drying the plates and tankards with a cloth and putting them back on the dresser.

'I am, but tonight I am off duty. I don't even have a gun with me. Open the door and see.'

Brigit nodded to her grand-maman to show she'd finished and threw herself on to one of the benches at the table as Colette opened the door. The soldier was almost as old as Colette and his watery eyes squinted into the kitchen.

'What do you want?' Colette asked.

'Let me in and I'll explain.'

Colette threw open the door and the man shuffled inside. He glanced at the table and he stopped. 'Oh, madame, that looks tasty.'

'All home-made,' Colette said. 'I am Colette Fletcher, and this is my granddaughter, Brigit.'

'A pleasure to meet you,' the man said and removed his cap. His eyes stayed fixed on the table.

'Would you like a little wine, cheese and bread?' Colette asked. 'There's a little too much for Brigit and me.'

'There's a little too much for half a dozen people,' Corporal Rudolf chuckled.

Brigit chewed her lip, annoyed. That had been careless. Colette spoke slowly, thinking of her explanation as she spoke it. 'It was meant to be supper for the farm workers,' she began.

'But one of them had an accident with a hay fork,' Brigit put in.

'By the time we'd bandaged his foot it was getting dark,' her grand-maman said.

'And the Gestapo don't allow French people out after dark – you have a curfew – so they had to run off to their homes before it got too late and you shot them,' Brigit finished.

The old man sniffed a wet drop from his nose. 'Back in the last war we had the Turnip Winter. In 1916 our bread was made with potatoes. Horrible. But that year we had a potato famine. So in the winter of 1917 our bread was made with turnips. Black turnip bread. Even worse. Our coffee was made from finest tree bark and acorns. Tastes disgusting, but it's all we've had. That's why we lost the war. It wasn't losing the battles. It was being starved till we gave in.'

Colette knew all about the turnip winter and the suffering German soldiers but said nothing except, 'So would you like some of my bread and cheese?'

'Yes, please,' the old man said and hurried to sit next to Brigit, who cut him a slice and buttered it.

'You seem a bit old for the ruthless Gestapo,' she said.

Corporal Rudolf chewed greedily and spoke through a shower of crumbs. 'The best troops are guarding the important places and the places where the French Resistance are active – trying to spy and wreck our factories. Bray was such a quiet place they just need someone like me to keep an eye on the town. Me and my boss, Major Strauss.'

'I'm sure you are worth ten ordinary soldiers anyway,' Brigit said.

'I am. But all that's about to change. Some French clown put a tree across the rail tracks and stopped a train. The Resistance are moving into Bray. I think we're about to receive a full brigade of Gestapo. The ruthless ones. Putting that tree on the track was a careless mistake. The Resistance will be crushed within a month.'

'And you?' Colette asked.

'Probably sent back to my job in Hanover. I'm a postman, you know?'

'So,' Brigit said carefully, remembering the facts, 'the Gestapo in Bray consists of an old soldier and a major… at the moment?'

'Plus a regular army unit of fifty men,' the old man added helpfully. Then he laughed. 'You should have seen the panic at the camp when they had reports of an enemy plane landing at the old airfield last night. Racing around like cats with tin cans tied to their tails.'

'Goodness,' Colette cried and held a hand to her mouth. 'Enemy agents, landed in Bray? We are *so* lucky we have you to protect us… except you don't have a gun.'

'The army are searching. The Gestapo will deal with them when they're caught.'

'Of course,' Brigit said. 'So why are you here – in Grand-maman's farmhouse?'

'Ah. That's personal. You see, in the last war I spent some time here. I fell sick with the influenza in 1918. They brought me here to recover and be treated by a wonderful doctor and his helper.'

'Doctor Weger and young Marius Furst,' Colette said.

Corporal Rudolf looked surprised, then slapped his forehead. 'Of course, you'd have been here at the time. But they were wonderful to me. I just wanted to come back and see how the old place was getting on.'

'Better than the last war. We aren't in the middle of the war zone this time,' Colette explained. 'No troops and lorries and tanks and guns rolling through Bray – no shells dropping on the town. So now you've seen it, and been well fed, you can go back happy?'

'Ah, no. I was hoping to see just one more thing.'

'Come back in the daylight and I'll show you around,' Colette offered.

'I don't want to trouble you. But before I get sent back I'd like one last look at the place where Doctor Weger saved my life.'

'Where was that?' Brigit asked.

'I'd like to look in the barn,' Corporal Rudolf Muller said.

And Brigit gave a silent groan.

Berlin

General Fischer was fat. His smart black uniform was cut from the finest cloth and the wide leather belt tried its best to hold in his bulging belly. But he was fat and his eyes looked out like little coals through folds of lard. He tapped on the map in his office.

'Colonel Roth,' he said to the pale-faced, hawk-nosed officer beside him. 'I had a phone call from the Gestapo message centre. It seems a train came off the tracks near this little town of Bray last week. What do we know about it?'

'Bray is a quiet sector on the Somme. We've never had trouble there before. The Gestapo have a Major Strauss in charge. A bus inspector before the war. He just has an old corporal to help. His report says there was a storm and an old tree branch fell on the line. And last night there were reports of a light aircraft landing near the town... the sort the British would use to land a special agent.'

General Fischer looked up sharply. 'A British agent? Why didn't you tell me at once?' he demanded and slapped a hand on his desk.

Colonel Roth picked his words carefully. 'I have the report here... sir. But it arrived late last night, and you were in a hurry to get to dinner.'

The general glared at him. 'I had to go to an important meeting... in a restaurant... with some of Herr Hitler's closest advisers. They think a lot of me. They wanted my opinion... as we ate dinner.'

'Of course, sir,' Roth said and tried to hide his sneer.

'Can we send a troop of real Gestapo men to investigate this landing?' asked the general.

'There's trouble in Lille,' replied Roth. 'We don't have any Gestapo units to spare. Major Strauss can deal with this for now. We'll send a unit to help him as soon as we have one to spare.'

General Fischer nodded and his three chins shook. 'Fine. We will let Major Strauss stay in charge of the sector for now. Just keep an eye on it, Colonel Roth. Keep an eye on it.'

Bray

Colette Fletcher picked up an oil lamp from the mantelpiece and handed it to her granddaughter.

'Go and see if there are any animals wandered into the barn, Brigit. We don't want the corporal gored by a bull,' she said, and smiled at the old soldier.

Brigit joined in the trickery. 'Oh, it's all right if *I* am gored then?' she snapped.

'The cattle *know* you,' her grandmother said. 'Get them out of the barn before I risk showing the corporal around.'

Brigit gave a great sigh. 'Oh, very well.' She hurried through the darkness to the barn. The Resistance group were looking at a map and arguing over the best place to destroy a rail line.

'An old man from the Gestapo is at the farm and he wants to look in the barn. He says he stayed in here when it was a hospital in the last war.'

'It's not safe to let him in,' Marie Marcel said.

'But not a problem,' Blacksmith Legrande said. 'There is a door at the rear. When he comes in the front, we can slip out the back.'

'Which is exactly why I said we shouldn't hide in an attic with no escape,' Brigit muttered.

'Let's go quickly,' Aimee said, and led the way out of the barn as they heard Colette and Corporal

Rudolf crossing the farmyard. Colette was speaking loudly to warn the agents they were on their way.

'Yes, this was a hospital for a few months,' the farmer was saying.

'Do you remember a boy? He helped Doctor Weger.'

'I remember him well. Marius Furst was his name.' She raised the lantern and shone it inside the barn. The only person in the light was Brigit.

'All gone, Grand-maman.' She shone the lantern around the barn while the corporal told his tale of falling sick and being nursed there.

'Glad I got to see it before I leave,' he said.

'We will be so sad to see you go,' Brigit lied. 'When do you leave?'

'I don't know yet. But I'm sure the Gestapo crack troops will be arriving soon,' the old soldier said.

After he had gone, Brigit turned to her grand-maman and said, 'So we don't have long to take a few risks and do as much damage as possible.'

'If only we knew when those crack troops were coming,' Colette muttered. 'Because when they *do* arrive those risks will be deadly.'

Chapter Twenty-Seven

'We can't throw another tree on the track'

Wednesday, 4 June
1941: Bray-on-Somme

Colette Fletcher shook her head. 'No, Blacksmith Legrande. We can't throw another tree on the track.'

'That's what is bringing a tough Gestapo force to Bray,' little Henri Caron said with one of his usual sneers on his thin little, mean little, sour-plum face.

The group had met in the barn the following night so they could watch the farm track and see anyone approach half a kilometre away. The single lantern threw a warm glow upwards, but the shadows made their faces look grim.

'I wasn't here when you did that,' Aimee Furst said. 'But the front wheels of the train hit the tree trunk and jumped off the track before it came to a halt. Is that right?'

The Resistance group nodded, glum.

'The Germans sent a message to the next station for help and the train was back on the track in four or five hours,' Marie Marcel said quietly.

'If we'd used one of your bombs,' Henri Caron said. 'That would have twisted the tracks and taken a lot longer to repair.'

'I did my best,' Blacksmith Legrande said like a sulky child.

'You did a great job,' Aimee said. 'But I was sent to show you how you could do even better.'

'Tell us,' Colette put in.

Aimee took the map they'd been studying the night before and spread it in front of the lantern.

'Let me tell you *how* SOE think it is best. Then *you* tell me *where* is best.'

They bent over the map, but Brigit, who already knew what her maman was going to say, kept her eyes on the dark track from the town to the barn.

'The Germans are very good at repairing their tracks quickly, especially where they run across flat fields. They can even put a locomotive back on the track if we derail it… as you saw. But what about if we send the train so far off the track it overturns and takes the trucks and carriages with it?'

'Plant a bomb,' Henri Caron said with a smug nod. 'Just like I said.'

'But some German patrol might hear the bomb and investigate. Or we'd have to hang around, wait for the train to get within a few metres and set it off. We might not have time to escape.'

Marie Marcel looked cross. 'So we want something that is silent but wrecks the train?' she sniffed.

'A magic bomb?' Henri Caron huffed.

'Something much simpler,' Brigit said quietly, looking back from the open barn doors. 'The rails are bolted to the sleepers with connector plates.

Undo the bolts and the train will charge off the track at full speed.'

'I have large spanners in my forge,' the blacksmith said. He looked brighter now. 'They'd do the job.'

'Thanks, Monsieur Legrande,' said Aimee. She pointed at the map. 'If we do it on a curve in the track, the train will be flung to the side and will probably turn over. If you know of a curve beside a ditch it will be a massive job to dig the locomotive out. When the locomotive comes off, the trucks will ruin the track behind it.'

Henri Caron leaned forward. 'I used to be a trainspotter when I was a boy. I know every centimetre of that line.' He placed a fine finger on the map. 'Leclerc Woods,' he said. 'It will crash into the trees. It'll take days to get rescue machines near the spot. The line will be out of action for a week.'

Aimee smiled. 'Henri, you are a genius,' she said.

'I know,' he replied with a shrug. 'So when do we do this?'

'Soon,' Aimee said. 'Why not tomorrow night?'

Thursday, 5 June 1941

Ragged clouds drifted over the moon as the saboteurs made their way around the edge of the town of Bray. They waited in an old shepherd's hut, silent. Blacksmith Legrande had slipped into the town to collect his spanner. If he were caught by an army patrol he would have no excuse for being out on the streets after dark. He would be taken to the army base and shot. Would he betray his comrades before he died? They didn't know.

They shivered as they waited, but from fear, not from cold. Brigit's fear melted away when the blacksmith came panting over the field. They were going to act against the invaders. This was what she'd come to France for. Her heart raced with excitement.

Henri Caron led the way to the west of the town. The old houses and shops stood silent and grey. If there were army patrols out tonight they were as quiet as the bodies in the churchyard. They already knew the old corporal was off to his bed for the night.

Still Brigit's eyes strained in the dark in case a soldier was watching from the woods, or lying in the grass waiting to shoot anyone who moved. The girl shook her head. She was imagining it. 'I hope we don't get lost,' she whispered to her mother.

But Henri Caron needed no map. It was a long walk, sometimes stumbling over uneven fields still damaged by shells from the war of more than twenty years before, sometimes finding a sheep track worn smooth in the grass. They didn't dare turn on a torch. The assault course back in Wales had made Aimee and Brigit fit for this sort of venture. Marie Marcel and Henri Caron struggled.

An angry owl flew over them, hooting and making Marie Marcel cry out. They walked on until they reached a fence and Henri told them to climb over it. The railway line on the other side of the fence gleamed in the broken moonlight as they reached the track. 'It's too straight here,' Brigit said.

'I know, I know,' Henri Caron snapped. 'We're not at the right place yet.'

They stumbled over sleepers and slid on the gravel between them. It was worse than the fields. They arrived at a place where the track began to curve and the fields at the edge dropped away in a steep slope. 'Yes,' Aimee said. 'Perfect.'

The little newspaper reporter shrugged. 'It's like you said, Madame Furst. I am a genius.'

Blacksmith Legrande squirted oil from a can on to the four bolts that held the rail then placed the spanner, long as Brigit, on the nut. He paused.

'What is it?' Brigit asked.

'There's a tremor on the rail. The genius Henri forgot to check the railway timetables. There's a train coming.'

'The Germans don't publish their timetables,' Henri began to argue. But Marie Marcel grabbed him by the arm and said, 'Let's not fight among ourselves.' She dragged him down the slope towards the hedge at the side of a field.

The others followed, sliding through long grass in places, tripped by bramble branches in others. Now they could hear the fast thumping of the steam locomotive and the ground tremble. They were all wearing dark clothes and even if a driver had looked from his cab he'd have seen only bundles of cloth. The train roared above them with a screaming of metal as its weight was thrown against the curve. Brigit and the schoolteacher looked up.

'Coal wagons and petrol tankers,' Marie Marcel said. 'They'd have made a nice fire if he'd wrecked them in time.'

After a long while the ticking, clacking of the wagons faded and the group scrambled up the bank again. Blacksmith Legrande heaved against the spanner but it took all of them to help him push till the rusted nut began to turn. A warm breeze sprang up when they needed a cool one. By the time they had released all four bolts they were sweating. The blacksmith used the spanner like a lever to force the rail away from the joint. The weight of the train would do the rest.

'Let's get back,' Aimee said.

Marie Marcel looked at her fiercely. 'I think we should wait to see if it works.'

'We will risk being caught,' Aimee said.

'Who put you in charge?' the teacher snarled.

'I thought you said we shouldn't fight among ourselves,' Henri Caron whined.

'She isn't one of us,' Marie Marcel argued. 'She was sent by Mr Churchill to spy on us. To make sure we spend his money well.'

'I was sent to help,' Aimee said, chewing her lip to keep her temper.

'We were doing fine without you,' the teacher said.

'We were,' little Henri Caron put in.

Aimee was about to reply when Brigit said, 'I hear a train.'

Her young ears had picked up the sound before the others in the group. 'If we stay here the train will fall on top of us,' Henri went on, with a little panic in his voice. He tumbled down the embankment and the others followed. They pushed through the hedge at the bottom and into the field.

'Further,' Brigit said. 'We need to get further away. If it's pulling more petrol tankers, the burning fuel could spray a long way.'

No one argued. They staggered over the rough grass till they were a hundred metres from the line. The moon came out enough for them to see the dull black locomotive against the purple sky as it came round the bend. Brigit's lungs were aching from running and she realised she was holding her breath. Aimee wrapped an arm round her shoulder and the saboteurs watched, wide-eyed and open-mouthed.

Chapter Twenty-Eight

'We're going to attack the Germans with pencils?'

First came the screaming of iron as the wheels of the powerful locomotive and its heavy line of trucks scraped against the rails. Then a creaking of tortured metal being twisted; the clank of couplings was drowned by the thunder of tons of metal rolling down the embankment of half a kilometre of train. There was a soft explosion of steam as the boiler burst and the rush of truck wheels as they spun off and rolled down towards the saboteurs.

'Run,' Brigit cried as she felt the breath of a rushing steel wheel against her cheek.

The Resistance group didn't need her to tell them that. They raced over the field and into the shadows of the woods before they looked back.

'Better than fuel trucks,' Henri Caron gasped. 'A trainload of tanks. There must be fifty at least. The German plans for them will be ruined.'

'And so will we if we don't move soon,' Aimee Furst said quietly. Hot coals from the ruined locomotive set fire to the grass at the bottom of the embankment. The flames leaped upwards to the first twisted tank and in a minute the fuel from it spilled down and sent a fireball into the air. That started fires further down the line and more tanks burned in a golden glow.

'I want to stay and watch this,' Blacksmith Legrande said. 'It's better than the fireworks on Bastille Day.' His face was lit by the orange glow of the flames and he looked shiny-eyed as a child.

'The tanks will come with ammunition boxes. When they explode they'll send the shells in all directions,' Aimee explained. And to prove her words right there was the sharp crack of the first shell exploding and sending shrapnel high over their heads. Then the rattling roar of more from the first ammunition box that crashed into the branches of the trees over their heads and showered them with twigs.

They ran through the wood and heard trees falling behind them as the sky over their heads was noon-day bright and sunset gold. They didn't stop till they reached Colette's barn, where they sat panting, joy filling their faces. Even Marie Marcel managed a smile. 'We'll do that again,' she crowed.

'We won't,' Aimee said.

The schoolteacher looked at her with poison in her eyes. 'We don't take orders from you.'

'You do if you want the money and the weapons and the radios to carry on the fight,' Brigit said. 'At least listen to what she has to say.'

Madame Marcel looked sulky and Henri Caron looked suspicious. Blacksmith Legrande just looked puzzled. 'It worked this time. It'll work again,' he grumbled.

Aimee spoke quietly. 'Charles, what would you do if you were a German?'

'That's easier for you to say,' Henri Caron sneered. 'Since you're married to one.'

Aimee kept her temper. 'You are a Gestapo commander in Bray and you see all those tanks wrecked. What are you going to do?'

'I'd try to find out who did it,' the blacksmith said.

'And?'

'Make sure it doesn't happen again.'

'How?'

'Use the army to guard the line.'

'Not the whole line,' Henri Caron said. 'It would take hundreds of troops.'

'So where?' Brigit asked, starting to see where her mother's thoughts were leading.

Marie Marcel sighed. 'The Gestapo will look at all the places on the line where the Resistance can make an accident happen easily. The downhill stretches with a sharp curve.'

'That's what I was going to say,' the little newspaperman said with a sniff. 'As soon as we try to unbolt the track we'll be caught. We'd be mad to try the same trick again.' Aimee said nothing.

'We need to try something different next time,' Marie Marcel said, nodding as if it were her idea.

'And I know just what it is,' Brigit said. 'We've brought some pencil bombs with us,' she added. The girl crossed the barn and found a box that had been hidden behind a straw bale.

'We're going to attack the Germans with pencils? How do we do that? Put it in their ears and push hard?' Henri Caron snorted.

'Wait and see,' Aimee said.

Brigit returned with the box, carrying it as gently as a tray of eggs, and opened it. 'The SOE call them Number Ten Delay Switches,' she explained, lifting a thin brass tube out. 'At this end is a glass tube full of cupric chloride. Underneath it is a striker on a spring. You just crush the copper section to break the tube of cupric chloride, and that starts to eat away at the wire holding back the striker. When the wire snaps, the striker shoots down the hollow centre of the detonator, it hits the percussion cap at the other end of the detonator… and boom.'

'Would we have time to escape if we set one off?' Marie Marcel asked.

'Oh yes. There are different timers – some are set to go off after ten minutes and some after a day.'

'That won't stop a tank,' Blacksmith Legrande said.

'No,' Aimee agreed. 'This is just the detonator. You have to put one of these delay switches inside some explosives.'

'And the Germans are just going to let us walk up to their supplies, plant a bomb, then run away?' Henri Caron asked with a harsh laugh.

'That's where my plan comes in,' Brigit said patiently. 'It was you that gave me the idea, Monsieur Caron,' she went on.

The little man's chest swelled. 'Yes, I am full of ideas. I am the brains of this group.'

'Pah,' Marie Marcel said with scorn. 'If your brains were explosives, you wouldn't have enough to blow your cap off.' She turned to Brigit. 'So what is your idea?'

'Monsieur Caron said he used to be a trainspotter. If I pretend to be a trainspotter I can get close enough to the engines to plant a bomb. No one is going to suspect a girl with a notebook, collecting engine numbers.'

'They are,' the reporter said with a sigh. 'I went trainspotting for twenty years from the age of seven and in all that time I never saw a girl collecting numbers.'

Brigit shrugged. 'Fine. Then I'll have to become a boy.'

Chapter Twenty-Nine

'I know trouble when I see it'

Friday, 6 June 1941: Berlin

General Fischer sat at his office desk. Colonel Roth stood to attention at the other side. 'Bray, Colonel. You told me it was a quiet sector.'

'That's what our Major Strauss said, sir,' Roth replied, and jerked his chin upwards nervously.

'A second train accident in a week. A shipment of tanks destroyed. And does Strauss still say there are no Resistance workers operating in the Bray sector?'

'Yes, sir. He visited the engine driver in hospital …'

'The engine driver?' Fischer growled. 'A train and fifty tanks were destroyed yet the driver survived?'

'Yes, sir. It seems the driver heard a driving wheel crack and the whole engine shuddered. He knew it was going too fast to stop with all that weight pushing it downhill. He told the fireman to jump and he leaped after him.'

'A German driver?'

'No, sir, a French crew.'

Fischer slammed a meaty fist on the desk. A tray of pens rattled. 'Even more suspicious.'

'It could be an accident, sir.'

'Two in a week, Colonel Roth. Two in a week. Have a team of Gestapo men ready as soon as you can. One more "accident" in Bray and we send them in. Not bus inspectors and pensioners. I want killers. Ruthless killers.'

'We don't want to upset the local people, sir. Sending in a brutal gang could turn them against us.'

Fischer leaned forward and strained against his tight black uniform. 'Wrong, Roth. We do not want to upset Herr Hitler. We are invading Russia in the east. Millions of men are taking part. He is too busy to bother about the people of Bray. But if he hears about fifty precious tanks being wrecked he may just ask you, and me, and Major Strauss how that could happen. So, Colonel Roth, do you want to risk turning the people of Bray against us? Or turning Herr Hitler against us?'

'Understood, sir,' Roth replied with a click of his brilliant black boots.

Bray

Brigit walked through the empty streets of Bray. She came across an old woman on her doorstep. 'Where is everyone?' Brigit asked.

'Are you a stranger, lad?' the woman asked.

'Just visiting my grand-maman,' Brigit said quickly.

'The workers left at sunrise,' the woman explained. 'And the shoppers won't leave their homes till they hear the shops have something to sell. They're too afraid to be seen outside.'

'Why?' Brigit asked.

The old woman looked at her as if she were stupid and spoke slowly. 'Everyone knows about the German train that was wrecked last night. We're just waiting for the Gestapo to arrive and punish the innocent as well as the guilty.'

'They will try to catch the Resistance workers ... but they won't harm the ordinary people.'

'Ha,' the woman spat. 'Haven't you heard about the village in Central France – Oradour-sur-Glane? Six hundred and forty-two French men, women and children were killed in just a few hours.'

'No I haven't heard about that,' Brigit said quietly. 'What happened?'

'The Germans were angry at the way the Resistance was sabotaging their supplies. The local Resistance even had the nerve to kidnap a German officer. The Gestapo acted. The women and children were locked in the church and the enemy placed a fire-bomb beside it. When it was lit, two hundred and forty-seven women and two hundred and five children died.'

'How terrible!' Brigit gasped.

'One survivor lived to tell of the horror. She was called Marguerite. She escaped through a rear window of the church, followed by a young woman and child. All three were shot, and two of them died. Marguerite crawled to some pea bushes and stayed hidden overnight until she was found and rescued the next morning.'

A cat joined the woman on the doorstep and she stroked it. The sun was warm, but the houses seemed to shiver with fear.

'But we must fight the invaders,' Brigit argued.

'Why?' the old woman asked. For the first time she looked up at the child and squinted. She showed her pink and toothless gums. Before Brigit could think of an answer she went on. 'Not everyone agrees with you. Some people in this town want to just keep their heads down. Survive. Wait for the war to end then carry on like before. And some people in this town will happily tell the Gestapo who the Resistance workers are.'

'Would you?' Brigit asked quietly.

'No, lad, I won't betray you. I'm just saying, trust nobody. Now get about your business and if the Gestapo knock on my door I'll forget I ever saw you.'

'I haven't done anything wrong,' Brigit objected.

'Not yet, you haven't. But you've mischief in your eyes. I've seen three wars now – I was your age in 1871 when the Germans beat us – and I know trouble when I see it. Now be on your way.'

Brigit looked around anxiously. The dark windows of the houses and cottages seemed to be watching her. If the old woman knew she was planning something, then who else did? She could turn around and go back. Blacksmith Legrande would understand, but Marie Marcel and Henri Caron would say it proved that she and her mother were German spies.

The girl reached the railway station and walked past it to the depot where the trains were being loaded and shunted. She carried five lumps of explosive, each painted black to look like a lump of coal, and each with the tip of a pencil bomb sticking out, ready to be crushed. They were all on a twelve-hour timer. They would go off at around midnight.

'Put them in the fire door of the engines before the drivers light the fire,' Henri Caron had told her. 'No one will notice an extra lump of coal in there. And it will blow out the back of the boiler.

It will take weeks to fix each one. Pick the largest engines – not the little shunters. The big locos are the ones that pull the supply trains.'

'What if someone lights the fire before the timer goes off?' Brigit asked.

The reporter gave a wheezing laugh. 'Then they'll be blown up with the engine. And serve them right. If it's a German driver then he's the enemy. If it's a French driver then he shouldn't be working for them, should he?'

But Brigit was shocked to think her bomb could kill a Frenchman. Before she left Colette's farm she wrote five notes, in French, with a heavy charcoal stick. Each one read:

My friend, if you are French do NOT light this engine fire before morning.

So it didn't look odd, she added:

The firebox needs a small repair and is dangerous.

She would stick the notes on the doors to the firebox and hope the French drivers would understand.

She began to cross the lines towards the engine shed. 'What are you doing, boy?' a voice asked. 'Get off the lines. There are trucks being shunted back and forth all the time. Have you ever seen someone crushed between two trucks? Not pretty.'

Brigit turned to see a man in a soot-stained, navy-blue uniform and cap. He had blackened hands and grease and ashes on his cheerful face. 'I just thought I'd try and collect some engine numbers,' she said quickly.

'Then come to the back of the shed and I'll show you around. What's your name, son?'

'Call me Thomas,' Brigit said.

As they walked by the old blackened brick of the shed the man chatted. 'I'm Albert Moreau. And you remind me of one of my sons, Martin.'

'How many sons do you have?' Brigit asked.

'Three sons and two daughters, all fine young people,' he replied proudly. 'But none of them interested in trains. It's good to see a boy who is.'

Brigit nodded and they entered the cool gloom of the shed with the sharp scent of burned coal that made her eyes sting.

The man patted the two-metre-tall wheels of the first locomotive. 'This is a four-cylinder compound 4-6-0 no. 230.637. One of the Ouest series 2701–2820 built between 1908 and 1912. But you probably know that better than I do, Thomas. I can see you love trains.'

'I do.'

Albert Moreau gave a great sigh. 'Last night the Resistance wrecked a train carrying German tanks, you know?'

'I heard,' Brigit said.

The engine-driver lowered his voice. 'I have to work for the enemy, so I don't mind their supplies being damaged. But that locomotive was one of ours... a class 40 TA. I drove her many times and I was close to tears when I heard they'd destroyed her. But that's war.' He sniffed. 'Want to look inside the cab?'

'Oh, yes please,' Brigit said, and he lifted her up on to the footplate. She took in the maze of pipes and levers, dials and handles. To her joy the fire door was open. Before the driver could climb up to join her she pulled a piece of fake coal from her pocket, squeezed the copper tube till the cupric chloride was released, then threw it deep inside the firebox. In twelve hours it would explode.

Monsieur Moreau climbed up beside her. 'I'll show you some of the other locomotives now. I have a few hours before I leave. Just time to run home for supper before I fire up my engine.'

Brigit looked out of the cab window at the dozen locomotives crowded into the shed. 'Which one is yours?' she asked.

'Ah, this one is,' the man said with a smile and patted the engine where she had left the bomb. 'I love her as much as my children.'

Brigit groaned. And she wanted to scream.

Chapter Thirty

'You leave in a coffin or not at all'

'What's wrong?' Albert Moreau asked, seeing Brigit hold her head in her hands.

'I've just thrown a bomb into your firebox. It will explode at midnight – unless you light the fire first and then it will blow you up with it.'

The driver shook his head. 'So why are you telling me?'

'I thought we were just destroying machines, I never meant to kill my own people.'

'Then I shall have to make sure you do a better job,' the man said eagerly. He reached into the firebox and pulled out the bomb. 'There are quite a few engines in here that won't be leaving before morning. I know which ones they are. How would it be if I planted your bombs in them? They'll go off in the night, no one will be hurt, but the German supplies will be badly hit.'

Brigit looked up at his soot-smudged, kindly eyes. 'Why would you do that?'

He shrugged with both shoulders. 'For the same reason as you. I don't like being told what to do by the invaders... but I don't want to kill anyone, Thomas.'

Brigit held out a hand. 'I am proud to shake your hand, Monsieur Moreau. And you can call me Brigit.'

He grinned. 'I thought you were an odd sort of boy.'

*

That evening, when the saboteurs met in Colette's barn, Brigit spoke first. 'I have planted the bombs. They will explode at midnight.'

'I'll go and watch,' the blacksmith chuckled.

'Better not,' Aimee said. 'The Germans don't know we have these pencil timers. They will look for anyone who was hanging around the engine sheds at midnight.'

The others nodded.

Brigit went on, 'But I almost killed a man today.'

Henri Caron looked up sharply. 'Aren't we supposed to do that?'

'Not Frenchmen,' the girl said. 'Anyway, I thought soldiers were the ones doing the killing. We're just here to make the job of the German soldiers harder.'

'Mr Churchill didn't send us to kill the invaders,' Aimee put in. 'He certainly never thought Brigit would be do any killing.'

'But we killed the engine-drivers on the tank train,' Henri Caron objected. The light from the oil lamp lit him from below and the smoke made him look like a devil fresh from Hell. 'Who knows if the driver and his fireman were French or German?'

'I do,' Marie Marcel said quietly.

The others looked at her in surprise. 'What were they?' the blacksmith asked.

'They were French.'

'But…'

'How did I know?' the teacher asked. 'What do you think I do all day? Sit at home knitting socks for soldiers? Planting potatoes for victory? No. I go around and talk to people. In my time I taught a thousand boys and girls at the college. Most of them still live around Bray. I visit them or meet them in the cafés that are still open. We talk about the old days and we talk about what they are doing now. Some are working for the Germans because they must. Some work for the Germans because they believe they will rule us forever and we may as well make friends.'

'Collaborators,' Henri Caron hissed. 'When the war is over they will pay for their treachery.'

Marie Marcel shrugged her narrow shoulders. 'Some of my old pupils pretend to work in places like the factories, but they do as bad a job as they can.'

'What has that to do with the train crash?' Aimee asked.

'One of my pupils, Jacques Defarge, was having a coffee and I started talking to him about his job.

He said he was taking a locomotive to Amiens to collect a train of important German supplies. He said he hoped the Resistance would put a log on the line and wreck it.'

'But he could be killed in the crash,' Brigit said.

'I said that if the Resistance heard about Jacques' train, they might just arrange it,' Marie Marcel went on. 'And they'd do it at Leclerc Woods that night. The lad looked at me and he knew what I meant.'

'What are you saying?' Blacksmith Legrande asked and his low brow wrinkled.

'I'm saying that Jacques knew that I could arrange it. I told him the woods near Leclerc would be a good place for the Resistance to strike, and when.'

'I told you that,' Henri Caron said. 'We agreed it the night before. You betrayed our plan. You betrayed us all!'

'Don't be foolish, Caron,' the teacher snapped. 'Sooner or later we have to trust someone. I had to give him some idea of when and where the crash would happen, so he could be prepared to get off the train before it killed him.'

'Did he make it?' Brigit asked.

'He broke a leg. I saw him in hospital this morning. He was quite happy to have a few months off driving trains for the invaders.'

'I still say you put our lives at risk,' Henri Caron grumbled.

'Brigit risked her life this morning planting bombs in engines. If you are afraid to do what a *child* can do, then leave the group.'

Blacksmith Legrande jumped to his feet. 'No one leaves,' he roared. 'You leave in a coffin or not at all.' His face turned red with rage. The group fell silent. The blacksmith looked around. He lowered his voice. 'No one leaves,' he repeated and sank back to the floor in the circle of lamplight.

'Thank you, Charles,' Aimee said. 'Now, can we agree on our next target? And do we agree we want no French people hurt?' They all nodded. 'Then I have an idea.'

The saboteurs turned towards her.

'Let me tell you something that I remember from the last war. We were living in the farm when the German lorries arrived. By the end of the war they were making a terrible noise because they had no tyres left. Germany was running out of rubber. There is a tyre factory on the other side of Bray. If we can destroy it then it will be a big blow to the invaders.' She looked across at the teacher. 'Do any of your pupils work in the Albert factory?'

'Perhaps,' said Marie Marcel. 'But I can't just walk up to the factory gates and ask, can I? The Germans will probably have it guarded anyway.'

'Today I pretended to be a trainspotter,' Brigit said. 'What if I pretend to be a pupil at the college? I could say I was doing a project on rubber and wanted the factory to tell me about how it works?'

Aimee smiled. 'You could make a plan of the factory and the best place to plant a bomb,' she said.

'While I talk to the workers and see if there are any of my old pupils who might leave a door unlocked at night,' Marie Marcel said.

'Do we all agree?' Aimee asked.

'It is a great plan, but do we have time?' Henri Caron said. 'I've heard the Gestapo are preparing to send in a fresh set of men. Hard men who will root out the saboteurs. When they hear about the locomotives being wrecked in the engine shed, they'll know we're here and won't delay it any longer.'

'Then we have to do as much damage as we can while we still can,' Aimee said. 'Then we'll take a break and make sure Bray is the most peaceful town in France, till these hard men go away.'

Blacksmith Legrande sighed. 'The Gestapo don't scare me,' he said.

'They scare me,' Henri Caron whispered. 'And sometimes it's being scared that saves your life.'

Chapter Thirty-One

'Our lives will be much harder from now on'

Night fell, and the German curfew kept the people of Bray off the streets. Corporal Rudolf made his weary patrol around the moon-shadowed streets. A pair of soldiers from the army camp had been sent to help. But it was a punishment for them, so they spent as much time resting in the warmth of the church as they did looking out for saboteurs.

The Bray Resistance group had agreed to stay away from the engine sheds, but they made sure they were looking from the highest windows they could find when midnight drew near. Brigit, Aimee and Colette had a clear view of the town from the farm on the hill. They watched silently.

At two minutes to twelve they saw an explosion blast the roof off the engine shed and send red-tipped golden flames upwards to scorch the clouds. Moments later they heard the explosion and then the crashing of metal as wheels and cogs and sheets and rods of metal rained down.

The army camp alarm sirens sounded and by midnight the camp's single fire engine was clanging through the streets of Bray to help. No sooner had they arrived than the second of Brigit's bombs exploded then the third. The fire crew stood well back, afraid to get too close to the burning shed in case there were further eruptions.

These came at ten past and quarter past midnight. Still the Germans backed away while the shed burned and everything inside was ruined.

Water from the River Somme was pumped on to the shed and it saved more sparks spreading fire into the town. But nothing could save the engines inside and some coal trucks in the shunting yard started to burn too.

By morning a heavy, oily cloud of slate-grey, soot-specked smoke hovered over Bray. The Resistance group were mostly asleep by then. An old woman sat on her doorstep and shook her head. No one remembered her name. The people of Bray just knew her as Tante… Auntie. 'I warned the lad. I said this would mean trouble. And trouble will come. Again.'

Saturday, 7 June 1941: Berlin

General Fischer's face was usually the colour of unbaked bread dough. This morning it was strawberry-pink with rage. 'So what excuse has Major Strauss given this time? Did one of Mr Churchill's bombers fly over Bray, drop a single bomb on the railway shed then fly home again without anyone seeing it?'

'No, sir. The major did say the engine shed had old electric wiring and that could have started a fire that made a gas pipe to the lighting explode.'

'What complete nonsense,' Fischer roared. 'There were five explosions. Five. Were there five gas pipes to one shed, exploding one after the other?'

'No, sir.'

'No, sir, indeed. Two wrecked trains and now this. There is a Resistance group operating in the Bray sector. It is a new bunch of saboteur scum. You will go there and snuff it out before it grows and before it does any more damage. First you will shoot Major Strauss for letting this happen. Then you will root out the saboteurs and shoot them. Make an example of them. Shoot them one by one outside their pathetic little town hall where the rest of the town can see them. Then you will take twenty hostages. You will lock them away and say you will shoot them if there is another *accident* in Bray before we win this war next year. Is that clear, Colonel Roth?'

The tall young man gave a sharp nod and looked as if he'd been forced to swallow a box of pins. He saluted, turned smartly on his bright black heel and left the office. He hurried to his own office and picked up the telephone. He spoke quietly. 'Operator? Get me Major Strauss, head of Gestapo in the Bray sector.'

A minute later he was connected. 'I have some bad news, Uncle,' he said. 'Fatty Fischer has ordered me to take over your sector and root out the saboteurs in your area... Yes, I know you only have old Rudolf to help you, but the general isn't listening to any excuses, he still thinks you could have done more.'

Roth listened to the moaning man on the other end. 'Listen, Uncle, you are in danger. I know you think you're in Bray for a peaceful life, but that's all changed with these attacks... No, listen. My first order is to shoot you... Yes, I know it's not fair, but it's war. The only way I can save you is if you take some action before I get there with my troop. What sort of action? Well, arrest someone and execute them.'

Colonel Roth listened for a while and looked over his shoulder to make sure no one was listening. 'Wait, Uncle. We both know you have a spy in the Resistance group. A Resistance group that did no resisting till that British plane landed on Monday night. You must use your spy to betray the others – or even just one of the others. Best of all, get them to tell us where the British agent is hiding. If you can do that before I get there in two days' time, then it may just save you.' The officer took a deep breath. 'No more arguments, Uncle. Just do it.' And he placed the phone back in its cradle with a bang.

Chapter Thirty-Two

'I just didn't see you'

Bray

Brigit held a pencil bomb and for the fifth time showed Blacksmith Legrande how it worked. 'I can come with you,' she offered.

'No,' the giant blacksmith said as his thick sausage fingers struggled to grip the small copper tube that would set the timer working. 'I want to do this myself. I want to do this for France.'

'You wrecked the tank train,' Brigit reminded him. 'All of us together couldn't have turned the bolts on the track that loosened the rail.'

He nodded his shaggy head. 'But I had you with me,' he said. 'One day I may have grandchildren. When they ask me what I did in this war I want to tell them something I did alone.' He looked shyly at the girl. 'I don't want to tell them I unfastened a few bolts. Do you understand?'

Brigit rested her hand on his wrist. 'I think so.' But she worried that he might get it all wrong and be caught.

'The others all agreed it was my turn,' the man said.

'This timer is set for just fifteen minutes. You have to plant it and get out quickly.'

'I know.'

He slipped the pencil bomb into his pocket and shifted the canvas bag of tools on to his other shoulder. If he was stopped, he would say he was on his way to do an urgent repair job on a heavy-lifting chain at the tyre factory. The plan to plant a bomb would have to be abandoned.

He set off down the street towards the edge of town where the tyre factory stood with its tall chimneys and the stench of hot rubber wrapped around it like a blanket.

Brigit followed a hundred metres behind. At five o'clock, a hooter sounded, then a dozen men and women trudged out of the factory and through the high iron gates. The last man, the nightwatchman, entered a small hut not much bigger than a sentry box at the front gate. He turned his back and looked eastwards towards the hills as if he was in a daydream.

Blacksmith Legrande marched behind him and into the factory. 'Good evening, Victor,' he said.

The nightwatchman slammed his hands against his trousers and made a cloud of black dust rise from them. 'For goodness sake, Charles, I am not supposed to *see* you. You are on a secret mission and it's not very secret if you go saying good evening to everyone you meet.'

'Sorry, Victor, I forgot.'

'It doesn't matter now, Charles. Just get inside and do what you have to do.'

'Thanks, Victor. It's good of you.'

The nightwatchman was old and bent-backed, but he pulled himself up as straight as he could and cried, 'It is not *good* of me because I haven't *done* anything for you.'

'You let me in.'

'No, I did *not*. I just didn't see you… I mean, I just didn't see the man or woman who slipped into the factory while my back was turned.'

'Right. But it's not a woman. It's me.'

'I know… I mean, I don't know because I haven't seen you.'

'Right.' The blacksmith took a few paces forward then turned. 'How's your wife, Victor? My wife says your Mathilde hasn't been too well?'

Victor finally turned around and even a hundred metres away Brigit could hear his desperate voice. 'Go in, Charles. Go in, please. Don't say another word.'

'I was just…'

'Not another word, old friend. We shall meet in the café tomorrow and I will buy you a brandy if you go now and don't say another word.'

'Right.'

The blacksmith strode down the path to the main doors of the factory. They were a shabby green and large enough to let the lorries in and out. He took a long lever from the canvas bag and forced the padlock off the doors. They agreed that it would look suspicious if the German firefighters arrived to find the main doors into the factory had been left unlocked.

Wood splintered, then Brigit saw the doors open and the blacksmith disappeared inside. Fifteen minutes later he swaggered out, looking very pleased with himself.

'Good night, Victor,' Legrande said with a wave to the back of the nightwatchman.

'With any luck I will have a very *bad* night,' the man said.

'Why is that?'

'Because the factory will catch fire and it will take hours to put out the piles of burning tyres.'

'I suppose so,' the blacksmith said and began to walk back towards where Brigit was waiting. The tool bag clattered heavily against his leg.

'You were in there a long time,' the girl said as she skipped to keep pace with the man's long strides.

'Yes, well, there were lots of good tools in there. It would have been a shame to leave them in the fire. So I borrowed them.'

Brigit stopped. 'You looted the factory before you set the bomb?'

'Don't be silly. I set the bomb first and *then* I bagged the best tools.'

'But you were in there a quarter-hour. That means…' the girl began. She was interrupted by the explosion that came from the factory just a hundred and fifty metres behind them. 'Run, Monsieur Legrande. Run for your life.'

*

'Where is Marie Marcel?' Aimee asked as the group met in the barn later that night.' They had spent the sunset hour watching the filthy cloud of burning rubber hover over the town like the wings of a black angel.

'Maybe she's had trouble getting here. The town is swarming with German soldiers making sure we obey the curfew,' Blacksmith Legrande said. 'And they're all in a foul mood. This afternoon one came to my forge and said it wasn't a soldier's job to patrol towns and guard against women and children.'

'And I suppose they'll have to give up their sleep to do it too,' Henri Caron said.

'It's only till the Gestapo squad arrives,' Marie Marcel panted as she hurried into the barn.

'You're late,' the newspaper reporter said sourly.

'I had to go three kilometres out of my way, through the fields, to miss the patrols,' she said calmly. 'Those engine-shed bombs were a great success, and the tyre factory was too. Well done, Charles,' she said to the blacksmith, who beamed. 'But our lives will be much harder from now on,' she warned.

'Yes,' Aimee said. 'With the Gestapo due to arrive any day, I think our next sabotage should be the last for a while. We'll do it tomorrow night. Then we lie low.'

'So what will it be?' Blacksmith Legrande asked. 'A huge bomb?'

'No. Something much simpler.' She pulled out their map of the region and they all leaned forward to look.

Chapter Thirty-Three

'Do something or do nothing'

'The Germans made a mistake,' Aimee said. 'Mr Churchill's SOE spotted it and that's why they sent me.'

'And me,' Brigit muttered.

'Sorry. That's why they sent *us*. Bray looks like a dot on the map, but it's on the route from northern Germany to Paris.' She traced a line on the map with her finger. 'If we wreck that route then they will suffer. They should have guarded it better.'

'They will soon,' Marie Marcel put in.

'The rail service will take weeks to repair. But there's one more thing we can do before we take a rest.' Again, Aimee placed a finger on the map. 'Just here is a line of telephone and electric poles. And at this point – pole number 273j – the line divides to north and south Bray. If we take down just one pole – pole 273j – they will be without power or telephones for a couple of days. The army camp will be in chaos and so will the airstrip. They won't be able to talk to Paris or Berlin except by army radio. It will be a fine greeting for the new Gestapo unit.'

'But it won't stop the Gestapo. They will arrive, and they will punish the people of Bray. It will be our fault.'

'We've thought of that,' Brigit put in. 'Maman and I will leave a trail that will show we are to blame – the SOE from Britain, not the local people.'

'They'll shoot you!' Blacksmith Legrande cried.

'By the time the Gestapo arrive we'll have flown back to Britain. We will stock up with new supplies and come back in a few months' time,' Aimee explained.

'You'll run away and leave us to take the punishment?' Henri Caron said bitterly.

'Tomorrow, while I take out post 273j, you will all be at the church service. Everyone in Bray will see you. There will be army guards outside the church door. Chat to them. Make sure they know you were there when the power line was sabotaged.'

Blacksmith Legrande, Marie Marcel and Henri Caron looked unhappy with the plan. 'We should work as a team,' the reporter said. 'Someone to watch your back while you plant the explosives.'

'Brigit has better eyes and ears than any of us,' Aimee said. 'She will be my scout and warn me if there are any enemy in the area. We will do this tomorrow night. And the night after that a Lysander will pick us up and take us back to Britain.'

'You will be caught,' Marie Marcel said, and she sounded more like a schoolteacher than ever, lecturing a stubborn pupil.

'And if we are, we won't betray you,' Brigit promised.

'You could be shot.'

'We knew that risk before we even joined the SOE,' Aimee said. 'If we sit and do nothing then danger could come to us anyway. The people of Oradour-sur-Glane were shot for doing nothing.

Their crime was simply being French. At least we will be doing *something* to fight the enemy. After all, that's why we're all here.'

The others nodded.

'Mr Churchill told me Shakespeare said it best,' put in Brigit. 'He said, *"I must go and meet with danger there, or it will seek me in another place".*'

Blacksmith Legrande threw up his hands. 'Why are we all so gloomy?' He turned to Aimee. 'It is a good plan, Madame Furst. The Gestapo aren't here yet.'

Henri Caron nodded. 'The Germans will be guarding the railway tracks and stations.' He chuckled and rubbed his small hands together. 'I went around today as a reporter and interviewed some of the army officers. They seem to think there are at least twenty SOE experts in the district. They're in a panic. They think Mr Hitler will blame the army in Bray for the disasters. They can't wait for the Gestapo to get here and take over.'

'I need a drill, Monsieur Legrande. I will drill a hole in the post, pack it with explosives and set a sixty-minute timer for it to explode.'

'Sixty minutes?' the blacksmith said. 'Does that give you enough time to get away? The army will send troops to post 273j as soon as it falls.'

Aimee grinned. 'How will they send them?'

'They'll telephone the army camp and... oh, I see what you mean,' the blacksmith said and slapped his head. 'With the lines down, they will be very slow.'

Brigit nodded. 'We'll be safely back here before they find out what's gone wrong. And you will never have left the church service. We'll strike at eight tomorrow night when the patrols are tired and think their job is done. Now, get home and rest. We have a busy day tomorrow.'

The group left quickly, over the dark fields and the silent streets. They made dark grey shapes against the pale grey cobbles that glowed in a near full moon. Tattered posters flapped on the walls of the shops, advertising chocolate and petrol and shoes and magazines, perfumes and scented soaps they could no longer buy in the half-empty shops.

Outside the school the old corporal sat on guard, his rifle between his knees, half asleep and half on guard. One of the darker shadows crept towards him. The old man twitched and grabbed his rifle. The figure held up a hand to calm him, then whispered in his ear.

Berlin

'So, Uncle,' Colonel Roth said into the phone. 'You have heard about a sabotage attack planned for tomorrow night?'

'That's right, my boy. I wondered what I should do about it.'

Roth rubbed his weary, red-rimmed eyes and said, 'You have two choices, Uncle. Do something or do nothing.'

'And which do you think would be best?'

His nephew chewed on a knuckle to stop himself from screaming down the phone. 'Well, if you do nothing then that will be five acts of sabotage in just over a week, all in the sector you are supposed to be guarding. General Fischer in Berlin will hear of it. As soon as the new Gestapo squad arrive in Bray you will be relieved of your command. You will be stripped of your rank of major. A rifle will be placed in your hands and you will be put on the next train to Russia. There you will fight in the Arctic blasts and probably die.'

'I see. And if I act?'

'If you act then this saboteur will be captured. The new Gestapo squad will torture him, and he will tell us the names of all the Resistance workers in your area. You will be a hero. You will return to Berlin and be given a cosy desk job in a warm office.'

'It's a her.'

'What?'

'It's not a him, it's a her. My spy in the Resistance said that the saboteur tomorrow night is a woman. But I only have Corporal Rudolf to help me. He's half-blind, three-quarters deaf and wholly stupid.'

Rolf spoke slowly. 'Russian cold or Berlin warm. Even Rudolf is able to arrest some weak woman. Just *do it*,' he said and slammed down the phone.

Chapter Thirty-Four

'Think, Brigit, think'

Sunday, 8 June 1941:
Bray-on-Somme

The following evening, at twenty minutes to eight, Aimee and Brigit set off over the old sheep trails and cattle roads to the west of Bray town. The sooty scent of burning rubber and steam still stung their noses and eyes. The faint notes of the church organ drifted through the evening air.

'Tomorrow night we'll be heading for England. Are you looking forward to it?' Aimee asked her daughter.

'So long as I don't have to go back to my old school at Castle Bromwich,' she said grimly. 'Maybe a bomb will land on Mr Cutter and Miss Dennison.'

'Don't joke about it,' Aimee said sharply.

'Sorry, Maman.'

They walked on in silence. Foxes barked and little creatures squealed as they ran from swooping owls.

At last, Brigit and Aimee came to a string of poles stretched alongside a road. Brigit's lantern showed the nearest post was numbered 281n. 'Another eight poles to the west,' Aimee said.

Brigit's sharp ears heard a car in the distance. 'I think it's coming this way,' she said.

'In which direction?'

'From the town.'

Aimee dragged her daughter into a dry ditch and lay without breathing till it had driven past. It seemed to stop a half kilometre away then roared off on the road to Amiens.

'Let's go,' Aimee said softly.

They kept to the road till they reached a patch of woodland and a large pole at the edge of it. Young trees in the wood struggled towards the sky through the broken trunks of dead trees that had been shattered by the last war. The main power lines seemed to come out of the wood and divided at this point. The line they'd followed was behind them. Another line crossed the road and turned south.

'This must be 273j,' Aimee said. 'Blow this pole down and we cut the lines to both the north and the south.' She turned to her daughter, who was standing with her face raised, pale in the light of the almost full moon. 'What's the matter?'

'I don't know,' Brigit murmured.

Her mother shrugged. 'Stand a couple of metres into the woods, Brigit. In the dark where you can't be seen. And use those sharp ears. If you hear any cars or lorries coming, then whistle.'

'Yes, Maman,' the girl said and walked quickly past the first few trees and settled on the leaf mould on the ground. She strained her ears but all she could hear was the whirr of the hand drill that Aimee had borrowed from Blacksmith Legrande.

239

Brigit shivered, even though the night was warm and still. She breathed in the smell of pine and earth. And slowly it came to her. Post 273j stood where the road entered the woods. When they arrived at the post, Brigit had smelled petrol.

Petrol from the car that had passed them.

But she hadn't smelled it on the last hundred metres of the walk to pole 273j. She had only smelled it when they arrived. Why? Because the car had stopped there for a few seconds and the exhaust fumes had gathered in that spot.

She remembered hearing the car pause. Now she knew exactly where it had halted. Here. Why would a car stop at that spot on a quiet road with no houses for at least a kilometre?

'Think, Brigit, think.'

The Germans in the car hadn't stayed long enough to examine the pole, so why stop at all?

The drilling stopped as Aimee packed the explosives into the hole she'd made and there was a click as she bent the end of the pencil bomb to set the timer.

Brigit's mouth went dry with fear. The car had stopped long enough to let someone step out.

Who? A German guard? Why? Because they were expecting an attack on that very post at this exact time.

Brigit gave an urgent whistle. She heard another click, sharp and with the ring of iron. The crunch of army boots as a soldier stepped out of the trees just a few metres from where Brigit was hidden. Then a voice, speaking in French but with a strong German accent. 'Put your hands in the air and don't move, or I will shoot.'

Chapter Thirty-Five

'I'm not stupid, you know'

Aimee Furst looked towards the trees and saw the old corporal with a rifle pointed at her. She looked a little to his left and, with a nod, gave a signal for her daughter to save herself and hide. Brigit slipped back into the shadows and watched. Her mother said cheerfully, 'If I put my hands in the air then I will be moving, and if I move you will shoot me.'

'Eh?' the soldier said.

Aimee spoke as if she were talking to a child. 'You said don't move. I can put my hands in the air or I can stay still. I can't do both now, can I? Which do you want me to do?'

'Er. Turn around,' the man said. 'Right around to face me.'

Aimee turned slowly and found herself looking at a grey-haired man with faded-blue eyes in a wrinkled face. She gave him a wide smile. 'Good evening, Corporal, what can I do for you?'

The old soldier squinted at his captive. 'You can follow me to Gestapo headquarters and the major will have you shot. That's sabotage that is.' He nodded his head towards the telegraph pole.

'Not really. I was cold, and I was just taking a slice out of the pole to make a fire. I wasn't cutting it down.'

'I'm not stupid, you know,' the soldier said.

'Who told you that?' Aimee asked.

'I could shoot you right now,' he hissed.

'No, you couldn't.' Aimee sighed.

'Why not?'

'Because the safety catch is still on your gun.'

In the bat-black shadow of a tree Brigit gasped. She knew that when the soldier looked down at his rifle, her mother would jump forward and try to snatch it. But the old man was not *that* stupid. He snapped off the safety catch with his thumb. 'I used this in the last war, you know? I killed five hundred men in the Great War.'

'Ah, you were a cook?' Aimee asked. 'A very bad cook?'

The soldier jabbed his rifle at her. 'You won't be laughing when the major lets me shoot you,' he said. 'Now, move.'

He set off, boots clacking on the stony road. Brigit followed, treading on the grass at the side, silent as a hunting owl. Aimee walked in front of the soldier and he seemed glad of some company. 'Major Strauss is in the Gestapo, you know. They're the Fuhrer's secret state police. Ruthless they are. Ruthless. And the major will be so pleased to see you.'

'Why? Is he lonely?' Aimee asked.

'No, but there's been a lot of trouble in his district this past week. People like you wrecking trains and buildings, sending secret messages back to the British pigs. And it's his job to stop them.'

'He's not doing a very good job then, is he?'

'Exactly,' the old man cackled. 'His bosses in Berlin were going to sack him. Send him to join the army in Russia. Very cold is Russia. Major Strauss doesn't want to go, see? So if he has a French spy to shoot, it might just save his job.'

'I'm British,' Aimee said quickly. 'There is no French Resistance group in the area. That's why they sent me. The people of Bray are too afraid of you and Major Strauss. They're terrified of you. They refused to help me.'

'They have a good reason to be frightened of us. Just wait till the Gestapo hard men get here tomorrow.'

'Well, I *can't* wait,' Aimee pointed out. 'Not if you're going to shoot me tonight. So long as you tell them my corpse is British.'

'British? Even better,' Corporal Rudolf said. 'The major will be overjoyed to see you.'

'I'm so pleased to be making your major happy,' Aimee muttered.

'And you've made me happy too. Oh yes. He'll probably make me a sergeant for this. More pay. Better food. And I'll get to order a few men around. I can send them out on patrol while I stay warm in the barracks. Oh yes, we are both very pleased to see you.'

They marched down the road with just enough starlight to show the town of Bray ahead. When they arrived twenty minutes later, the street lights had been turned off and all the windows were shuttered and dark. A warden nodded to the soldier as he passed, checking for lights showing. 'Good evening, Rudolf,' he said.

Brigit was following a short distance behind and straining to hear her mother and the soldier talking. She hadn't seen the warden and threw herself behind a garden wall just in time. 'Careless girl,' she whispered to herself.

'Evening, Walter,' the soldier replied.

'Who you got there then, Rudolf?'

'French spy,' the old man said proudly. 'Says she's British, mind.'

'Really? Must be the major's first one. He'll be pleased.'

'Just what I was saying.'

'The major might let you shoot her... after she's told you all she knows,' the warden said. 'Have you ever shot anyone before?'

'Five hundred in the last war, he told me,' Aimee answered.

The warden laughed and leaned towards Aimee. 'Rudolf was a truck driver back in 1914. He delivered cabbages and turnips. He was too old even then to fight in the trenches.'

The soldier spoke angrily. 'I *trained* with the rest of the troops. I know how to fire a rifle, Walter. If the major wants me to shoot her I will. Now,' he said, waving his rifle at Brigit's mother, 'into the school. It's on the right.'

'I think I know where it is,' Aimee said quietly.

The soldier let her lead the way. 'Goodnight, Walter,' he called.

'Night, Rudolf,' came the reply. 'Good shooting.'

Chapter Thirty-Six

'We still have work to do'

Aimee and the old soldier reached the door of the school. 'It's an odd place to bring me,' Aimee said. She spoke loudly so her daughter could hear.

'It seems the school was the German army headquarters in the last war, so the Gestapo decided to use it again,' the corporal told her.

'I know that. But it's an odd place because it's not a prison. You can't lock me in,' Aimee went on.

The soldier lowered his rifle and waved a finger. 'That's where you're wrong, madame. There is an old book cupboard in one of the classrooms. The door can be locked and the only window is too small to climb out of. You'll be safe there.'

'Yes,' Aimee cried. 'The old cupboard on the north wall of the school. The little window is three windows along from the east corner. I should be snug in that book cupboard.'

'Plenty to read,' Rudolf chuckled. He didn't stop to wonder how Aimee knew the school so well.

The woman sighed as she took one look back into the starlit schoolyard. A small white hand waved from the school gate to show her that her daughter had heard and understood.

'In you go. Major Strauss will be dozing in his office chair, but he won't mind being woken up to meet a spy,' the old man said.

'I look forward to meeting him,' Aimee said quietly as she entered the cupboard and the smell of the dust was the same as it had been over twenty years before when she had been the spy-catcher. The old Latin books they had used were gone. The new ones were to teach the French children English. She wondered when they would be forced to learn German.

The books had been tumbled to the floor to make room for Gestapo notepaper and envelopes, files and pencils, pens, ink and blotting paper.

The door closed and the key clicked in the lock. A dim, yellowed bulb glowed from a frayed cord in the ceiling.

Aimee set to work lifting the books from the floor and stacking them to make a small stairway to the starlit window. The window frame had stuck from years of swelling in the winter rains. She took out a knife from her sock and began to cut through the old paint.

Sweat dripped from her brow and fell on to the dusty floor. Her hand was bruised with pushing at the handle but at last she felt the blade give way as it reached the outside. She used the knife as a lever and slowly the window began to creak open. She put the knife back in her sock… a good Gestapo officer would probably find it soon enough. She pushed at the window till it opened enough to let the fresh spring air into the musty space. 'Brigit?'

'Here, Maman,' the girl whispered from the narrow alley that ran down the side of the school. 'How will you escape?' she asked.

'I won't. Not yet,' she replied. 'We still have work to do.'

'Inside a book cupboard?' Brigit said, frowning.

'You will have to be my eyes, ears and feet for now,' her mother said.

'I can throw a pencil bomb through the front door. When they're picking the splinters out of their ugly faces, I'll rescue you,' Brigit promised.

'No, listen. That old guard didn't find us by accident. There are a thousand telegraph poles along the River Somme. How did he know which one we were planning to bring down?'

'Luck.'

'A thousand-to-one chance? *Thousands*-to-one if you think he didn't just pick the right place, he picked the exact time too. Luck? I don't think so. We were betrayed.'

'But only six people knew where you'd be at eight o'clock,' Brigit argued.

'Yes, and one of them is a traitor, working for the Gestapo.'

'So we need to get you out, Maman. And in time to catch tomorrow's Lysander flight back to Britain.'

'If we do that the traitor will carry on and betray everyone. The others – our brave friends – will be shot. So will your grand-maman, Colette. We can't allow that to happen.'

'Then we have to find out who the traitor is before we make our escape,' Brigit said slowly. 'How can you do that from inside a cupboard?'

'I can't,' her mother said simply. 'But you can. Take this notepaper and these envelopes,' she said, passing them out of the window. 'If you want to know where a rat is hiding, you put out a piece of cheese. This Gestapo paper is the cheese and you are going to set the trap. Listen carefully and I'll tell you how.'

Chapter Thirty-Seven

'We can't just leave her there to die'

Berlin

Colonel Roth fastened the buttons on his uniform and pulled on his long boots before he marched to the hotel where General Fischer was staying. The guards on the door saluted as he walked past them, and he hurried up the stairs to room 157. He tapped on the door.

'Who is it?'

'Roth, sir,' the colonel said.

It was a minute before the door opened. Red-faced General Fischer was brushing his thin hair over his bald head and peered up at his visitor.

'Roth, do you know what time it is?'

The colonel looked at his watch. 'Eight forty-two, sir.'

The general's face turned an unhealthy shade of purple. 'I wasn't asking you the time, I was asking you why you thought you could disturb me at this time of night.'

Roth feared the general's bulging eyes would pop from his skull. 'Sorry, sir, but it is very important.'

'It had better be.'

'It's Bray, sir.'

'Not another sabotage. If it is then I shall have your uncle shot…'

'But, sir.'

'No. I won't have your uncle shot, I will go to Bray and shoot him myself. Just let me get my uniform on and find my pistol. Call a car. I'll go there at once,' he said and stamped back into his bedroom.

'No. It's not another sabotage. I wanted to tell you that my uncle – I mean, Major Strauss – has arrested a saboteur in the act. A British SOE agent. He has her imprisoned at his headquarters.'

'He has? That buffoon Strauss has actually captured one of Mr Churchill's agents?'

'Yes, sir.'

'But that is wonderful news. Why didn't you telephone me at once?'

'But, sir…'

'Tomorrow I shall drive to Bray and question her myself… you said it was a woman, did you?'

'Yes, sir.'

'I always said that Major Strauss was a good man. There'll be a medal for him. Maybe one for me too, eh, Roth? What a hero old Strauss is. Always said it. Always.'

Bray

Brigit hurried down the main road as fast as she dared, afraid she might trip in the darkness. The case she was carrying mustn't drop or the plan would be ruined. Tuneless singing came from the church. She turned up a small lane and headed up the hill towards a farmhouse. A light glowed behind the shutters. Brigit knocked on the door.

Cattle snuffled in the field and owls hooted in a distant wood. At last a voice spoke from behind the door. 'Who's there?'

'It's Brigit, Grand-maman. Can I come in?'

The door opened quickly and Brigit stepped through the blackout curtain into the warm room. Colette Fletcher wrapped her strong arms round her granddaughter and kissed her head.

The girl was hurried inside and her precious suitcase laid gently on the old oak table. When her grand-maman had placed a bowl of chicken stew in front of Brigit, she asked, 'Where is your maman?'

'She was arrested and taken to Gestapo headquarters.'

'The school? Then we must contact the others and find a way to set her free.'

Brigit did her best to explain quickly. 'We can't. At the moment the Germans think Maman is the only Resistance worker in the area. If we raid the

256

school they'll know she is not working alone. When the new Gestapo troop arrives, they'll seek you out and shoot you all.'

'We can't just leave her there to die,' Colette cried. 'Let's see what the others have to say.'

'We can't do that either,' Brigit said. 'One of them is a traitor. Maman and I knew about tonight's plan. So did you. None of us told the Gestapo. That just leaves Blacksmith Legrande, Marie Marcel or Henri Caron. One of them is working for the enemy. We need to find out which one and *then* set Maman free.'

'I don't see how we can do that.'

'Don't worry. Maman has a plan. She said I'd be safe here while we put it in action.'

'Of course you will,' Colette said warmly. 'Now, let's get on with it.'

*

Just after nine o'clock, when she knew the saboteurs would have returned home from church, Brigit got ready to leave. She slipped three Gestapo envelopes into the pocket of her smock dress. Each one had a name written neatly on the front.

Brigit headed for the door. Colette had given her a small torch and made a rough sketch of Bray town. The girl was careful to look for Warden Walter in the grey streets under a grey moon. The warden was wearing army boots that clacked on the cobbles so as she made her way through the maze of streets she had plenty of warning.

She watched as the warden stopped at a cottage on King Street and rapped on the door. When it was opened he said, 'I can see a light through your curtains. Is that a signal for the British bombers?'

'There are no British bombers,' the Frenchman inside grumbled.

'No, but there will be as soon as they see that light. Now close your blackout curtains tighter, or turn out the light, or pay a hundred-franc fine.'

The door was slammed in Warden Walter's face, but soon after the curtain was shut tight.

There was a distant 'bang' as the explosives in the telegraph pole finally brought it down. The timer was late. Every light in Bray went out except in the oldest houses that still had gas and oil lamps.

Brigit followed the warden and at last reached the first mark on her grand-maman's map. Walter had turned a corner. She slipped an envelope under the door of Blacksmith Legrande, knocked and ran to hide in a doorway across the road to make sure the door opened and the huge man found the envelope.

Then it was the turn of the schoolmistress, Marie Marcel, on Zola Street. On over the moon-washed cobbles to Green Street, and the reporter, Henri Caron.

Then she went on to the church. Boughs on the old yew tree creaked in the evening breeze and Brigit shivered a little. 'There are no such things as ghosts,' she muttered to herself as she walked through the gate and found a gravestone to hide behind. It was one with a good view of the church door.

The clock on the church tower showed twenty-five past nine. Five minutes to wait.

*

Legrande took the envelope in his smoke-stained hand and swallowed hard. It had his name, written in ink, on the front. On the back it said

'Gestapo Headquarters, Somme District, The Old School, Bray'.

'What is it?' Madame Legrande asked as he held the letter up to a smoky oil lamp.

'A letter.'

'I can see that. What postman delivers letters at this time of night?' she snapped.

'Delivered by hand,' he replied, turning it over.

'What does it say?'

'Blacksmith Legrande.'

'Yes, but what does it say *inside*?'

'I don't know.'

'Why not?'

'Because I haven't opened it.'

Legrande's wife gave an impatient sigh. 'Don't you think you'd better? It could be important – in fact it *must* be important if someone delivered it at this time. Open it. Hurry up. I want to get to bed. We've had too many late nights.'

The blacksmith's powerful hands trembled as he placed a finger under the flap and opened it. He pulled out the letter as if it were a hand grenade with a loose pin and unfolded it. He read it aloud.

'Dear Legrande… that's me.'

'Yes, we know that. Who is it from?'

'Major Strauss, head of the Somme Gestapo.'

'Trouble.' His wife sighed. 'What does he say?'

'It doesn't make sense. He says that my work as a spy for the Gestapo is priceless. He has captured the British secret agent, thanks to my tip-off. He has a large payment for me and a new task, but I must not be seen at the school headquarters… and he must not be seen coming to my forge. He wants me to meet him at the church door at nine thirty tonight when he will tell me more. It's signed Major Strauss.'

'Is that his signature?' Madame Legrande asked.

'How would I know?'

The woman pulled a shawl tight around her shoulders. 'It's a trap. If you turn up at the church door at nine thirty then you will be admitting that you work for the Resistance. He's probably sent a hundred of these letters around Bray. There will be a whole troop of soldiers waiting with machine guns.'

'That's what I thought,' Legrande muttered.

'No, you didn't,' his wife said sharply. 'Just as well you have me as the brains in this family. So what will you do?'

'I will go…'

'Yes?'

'To bed.' He crumpled the letter and threw it on the last embers of the fire where it flared and died.

Chapter Thirty-Eight

'Good evening, madame. Take a seat'

Major Strauss had the buttons on his uniform fastened into the wrong buttonholes. His face was sour as crab apples in the smoky light of an oil lamp. 'Yes, Corporal Rudolf, I have phoned Berlin to tell the general about our capture – at least, I spoke to Colonel Roth when you brought Madame Fletcher back here. And, yes, he was sure there would be a promotion for us both. We could be posted back to the comfort of Berlin and cosy beds.'

Rudolf was shuffling from one foot to the other, waiting for the major to stop talking. 'And do they want us to question her?'

'It can wait till morning, can't it?'

'I have been thinking, sir…'

'At this time of night? Can't you save your thoughts till the morning? I'm tired.'

'But, sir, if there are any others in the Resistance, they will know something's happened to this British spy. When they find out we have executed her, they will scatter and we'll never find out who they are. We have to act now. Get her to tell us their names and send an army squad to arrest them before they know what's hit them.'

Major Strauss sighed. 'Yes, Rudolf, you are right.'

The old man appeared to glow and grow a few centimetres. 'I am, sir?'

'And if we uncover a nest of traitors, we'll end up with enough medals to sink a battleship,' the little man said and rubbed his hands. 'Let her out now.'

The corporal strutted out of the classroom that the major used as an office, across the hall and into the room with the cupboard. He unlocked it and opened the door by the light of an oil lamp. 'Come out. Hands up. Try to run and I will shoot,' he ordered.

Aimee Furst stepped out and smiled at him. 'Thank you, Corporal. It's good to stretch my legs.' She looked up at the unlit, fly-specked bulb.

'What's the matter?'

'Just checking to see that the bomb I planted under the power line went off. I see it has. I think maybe you should have inspected it *before* you arrested me.'

Rudolf turned pale. 'What bomb?'

Aimee gave a sad smile. 'When you arrested me, I was planting a bomb in the pole that carries the power lines. I managed to set the timer before you could stop me.'

'Set it? Timed for when?'

Aimee said with a shrug. 'It's gone off, hasn't it? Did you think it was just another failure at the power station? Well, it wasn't. It was sabotage and you let it happen. I'm guessing you'll be in trouble.'

'I'll shoot you,' the old soldier said, jerking his rifle towards her.

'You're going to shoot me anyway so why should I care? The bomb has gone off and the Gestapo in Berlin will be furious. Another act of sabotage in Bray that you failed to stop. They may even shoot you and your major when they arrive.'

Rudolf jerked the rifle again. 'Across the hall to the major's office,' he ordered. She obeyed.

Major Strauss was fussing with papers on a desk and looked up when Aimee walked in. He tried to look calm but blood was pounding in his throat and he had to loosen the collar on his black uniform. 'Good evening, madame,' he said. 'Take a seat.'

'You are very kind,' Aimee said calmly and sat opposite him.

'You are a British spy.'

'I am.'

'And you work with a Bray Resistance group.'

'No, I don't. There are no French people in Bray willing to work for the Resistance.' She leaned forward and looked the major in the eye. 'They know you are in charge. They are afraid of you. Mr Churchill knows of you and he knows this district is safe while you are in command.'

Major Strauss seemed to inflate like a peacock. 'Mr Churchill has heard about me?'

Aimee gave a soft laugh. 'Who hasn't? Strauss, the terror of the Gestapo, we call you. We tried to get the folk of Bray to rise up against you, but they refused, because of you. And then a strange thing…'

'What?'

'We decided to send an SOE agent into the town to sabotage the enemy supplies. And do you know how many of my SOE friends offered to come?'

'No?'

'Not one,' Aimee said. 'All too afraid. Afraid of the great Major Strauss.'

'I can understand that,' the major said and fluffed his peacock feathers still more. 'So you are telling me you acted alone?'

Suddenly Corporal Rudolf stepped forward. 'Excuse me, sir. She was alone when I caught her at the power line – the one that's just blown.'

'The lights went out over an hour after you arrested her.'

'She says it was on a timer, sir.'

'And you failed to stop her?' the major squeaked.

'I did, sir, but I just wanted to say she can't have acted alone on all the sabotages.'

'Why not?'

'Because of the tank train, sir. That took a huge effort to loosen the track bolts. It was either someone really strong, or a few people heaving on a long lever. She couldn't have done it alone.'

'Yes, Rudolf. I was just about to say that. So, madame... your name, by the way?'

'Aimee Furst. You can call me Aimee.'

'So... Madame Furst, the names of the Bray people who helped you, please?'

The door to the office creaked open and three pairs of eyes turned to see a girl standing at the door. 'Brigit?' Aimee gasped. 'This wasn't part of the plan,' she muttered.

Brigit fixed her eyes on the major. 'I have the names of the Bray traitors here,' she said, waving a piece of paper. 'The French people willing to join the Resistance now they've seen how Maman has done it.' On it were written three names:

Camille Olivier
Hugo Philippe
Bastien Robert

'You have betrayed these honest French people,' Aimee said with a soft cry.

'I had to, so I could save your life, Maman,' Brigit said.

'This is your daughter?' Major Strauss asked.

'It is.' Aimee nodded.

'Mr Churchill sent a child to fight with the SOE?'

'Churchill is a fool,' Brigit said, with as much venom as she could. 'Churchill never realised that Maman and I are both fighting for the true fatherland. For Germany.'

Chapter Thirty-Nine

'My dream... my wildest dream come true'

Brigit had delivered the letter to Blacksmith Legrande, Marie Marcel and Henri Caron, then hidden in the churchyard to see which one turned up. She wasn't surprised to see who it was. When the traitor had given up waiting and gone home, the girl hurried to the school and tiptoed through the door. It smelled of chalk and book dust, the teachers' cigarettes and the caretaker's floor polish. The scents took her back to her own school in Castle Bromwich and she shuddered.

She had stepped through the blackout curtain and stood by the door of Major Strauss's office. She waited for her maman to give her the cue to enter the room with the list of names.

Aimee shook her head. 'Brigit, you have given away our great secret. We were only supposed to tell it to Major Strauss's boss in Berlin.'

The little man jumped as if he'd grasped a live wire. 'General Fischer?'

'That's the name,' Aimee said.

'You have a secret for General Fischer? But you can tell it to me,' he said in a soft voice.

'Brigit's already told you I am working for Germany,' said Aimee.

'She's lying. Let me shoot her,' Corporal Rudolf said.

Major Strauss rose to his feet. 'You failed to defuse that bomb, man. If there is any shooting to be done, then it will be the general shooting you. He arrives tomorrow and if he finds your carelessness has wrecked the power and telephone lines it will be you facing the bullets. Get out. Drive to Amiens where you can phone Berlin with the latest report. Speak to my nephew, Colonel Roth, at Gestapo headquarters.'

Corporal Rudolf scuttled away and left Aimee and Brigit alone with the major. The girl looked sly. 'Now the old man has gone we can tell the major our secret can't we, Maman?'

Aimee threw her hands in the air. 'I suppose so, child. Strauss, the terror of the Gestapo, can be safely told…'

'Told what?' the man breathed.

Aimee leaned forward. 'I am a German spy. The SOE offered me the chance to join them because I was born in France and live in England.'

'So why would you work for Germany?' the major asked.

'Because my husband is German,' Aimee said simply.

'You are just saying that,' Major Strauss said, frowning.

Aimee gave a one-shouldered shrug. 'No. It is too easy for you to check. Berlin will have a list of all the Germans in Britain who are interned in their prison camps. You will find the name Marius Furst on the list of Germans in the camp at Castle Bromwich in the English Midlands.'

'I can't check. You've wrecked the phone lines.'

'Wait a moment,' Aimee said. She stepped outside the door and came back with a heavy book bound in dark red leather. She placed it on the Major's desk. 'This is the church record of births, marriages and deaths. Look at 20 April 1923.'

The Gestapo commander opened it and turned the pages. '1923,' he muttered and ran his finger down the columns. '20 April – Hitler's birthday... ah, here we are.' He read it aloud. 'Aimee Fletcher of Bray married Doctor Marius Furst of Germany?'

'Yes. But the people of Bray drove us out. They drove my poor husband away when he came here to help the sick. They drove me out of my own home. That's why I hate them. That's why I want to see France defeated. We went to England where we could spy if a war came along, and it has.'

The major nodded slowly. 'I see.' He looked up, troubled. 'But Madame Furst,' he said. 'You wrecked a trainload of tanks and an engine shed and a tyre factory, yet you claim to be a German spy?'

'The tanks were old models going to a scrapyard,' Brigit said.

'The trains were French puffers that will be replaced by powerful German ones,' Aimee put in.

'And the tyre factory was producing third-rate rubbish that wasn't fit to be seen on our fine German Mercedes cars,' Brigit finished.

'And the power lines?' Major Strauss said.

'One telegraph pole that you'll have back up in a couple of hours,' Aimee cried. 'But when the traitors in Bray see those actions they will flock to join the Resistance. That way you can round them up and arrest them. Strauss, the terror of the Gestapo, will have his greatest triumph.'

The major sat back in his chair and enjoyed the moment. 'And how do I... round them up?' he asked.

'Camille Olivier, Hugo Philippe and Bastien Robert will be in Bray churchyard tomorrow night at ten o'clock. I have arranged it. There will be others there with them. I don't have all of their names. But you could catch a dozen fish with one net,' Brigit promised. 'I'm afraid you will have to trust me until then... If the traitors see I've been arrested they will never crawl out from under their evil stones ever again. You will have to let me go right now.'

'It may be true that your German husband is interned in England as you say. My colonel in Berlin told me the Gestapo have planted a secret agent in Bray to betray any Resistance workers. There is just one thing that my nephew said that puzzled me.' The man rested his elbows on the table and leaned forward. 'The name the colonel gave me wasn't Aimee Furst.'

Aimee had been expecting that. 'Of course not. Aimee Furst is my real name. I gave it to you, so you could check I was telling the truth about Marius.'

'So what name have you been using?' the major asked.

And Brigit gave him the name of the Resistance worker who had appeared in the churchyard at nine thirty that evening.

The major beamed. 'Yes. That is the name my nephew gave me. Make sure the French rebels are all in the churchyard tomorrow at ten...' He stopped suddenly as he remembered. The man's mouth fell open and he stumbled over his words. 'But Colonel Roth said General... General Fischer... he's coming to Bray tomorrow. Coming here. Do you see what this means? He will be there to *see* my greatest triumph. He can watch as I round up the whole nest of vipers. Oh, my dream... my wildest dream come true. Madame Furst – and Brigit, of course – thank you, thank you.'

Brigit and her mother looked at one another. 'Our pleasure, I'm sure,' Brigit said. Aimee rose from the chair. 'We'll bid you goodnight then, Major Strauss. Sleep well. Tomorrow at this time your life will be changed forever.'

'Forever,' he breathed.

Chapter Forty

'I'll kill the evil turncoat'

Monday, 9 June 1941: Bray-on-Somme

Brigit slept well and woke long after the farmhouse cockerel had greeted the day. She swallowed her breakfast eggs too quickly in her excitement. By this time tomorrow she'd be waking in England... or in a Gestapo cell.

Aimee went off to the barn to collect the radio and take it to a place far away from the farmhouse. If the Germans could track the signal back to the farm, then Colette would be in danger. She walked into the hills above Bray where she had walked as a girl. She passed the drovers' road where she had led a young German soldier to safety at the end of the last war. The man who had returned and married her.

She stopped and sent a message to London about what had been happening. She switched off the radio after three minutes in case the trackers had spotted her. She knew it was unlikely.

She moved five kilometres further east to where some of the fiercest fighting of the last war had taken place by the River Somme. The shattered, shell-sunken, trench-torn fields and woods had repaired themselves well and the land looked rich and green. Far too rich to allow the invaders to steal it.

Aimee sent her second message, making final plans for that evening's flight home. 'A plane with room for a third passenger,' she finished. She closed the suitcase that held the radio and walked steadily back to the farm.

*

Brigit had gone into the town by then. The streets were filled with people complaining about losing their electric power. The poor folk, who couldn't afford electric, still used gas and they gloated a little. Most of the shops and factories had to close and the workers hung around the doors, chatting and waiting.

The streets were filled with German lorries, some carrying the remains of the broken train and tanks back to the army base, others going the other way to repair the ruined telephone and power lines.

Brigit found Blacksmith Legrande in his forge, where he pushed at bellows to make the coals glow white-hot and crafted metal rods. He looked up and smiled. 'Busy?' Brigit asked.

'Busy making new fittings for the power lines. Someone brought a big pole crashing down in the early hours.'

Brigit let her mouth go wide in mock shock. 'Really? Who could do such a thing?'

'The gossips say there is a British spy in Bray hoping to set up a Resistance group,' the blacksmith said and gave the girl a large wink.

She moved closer to the man and felt the scorching heat of the forge. He dipped the hot metal into a pail of water where it hissed and spat and turned from red to black. They moved away from the forge and the blacksmith cleared a space on a bench cluttered with horseshoes and nails, brackets and metal bars, so they could sit down.

He spoke as softly as his growling voice would allow. 'I had an odd letter last night,' he said.

'I know,' Brigit said. 'I posted it through your door.'

The man blinked. 'But it was from the Gestapo. Are you working for them?'

'Of course not. Maman was betrayed. Someone in our group told Major Strauss of our plan to bomb the power lines. I sent a letter telling each of you to go to the churchyard at nine thirty last night.'

'I didn't go,' the man said.

'Of course you didn't. Because you're not the traitor. Only the one who really is working for the Gestapo was going to turn up. And I was there to see who it was.'

'And who was it?' Legrande asked.

Brigit told him.

'I'll kill the evil turncoat,' the blacksmith growled and gripped his heaviest hammer.

'Then the Gestapo will know there is a Resistance group in Bray. They *think* there is just a single SOE agent here from Britain. What we must do is make the traitor vanish. As if they got scared and ran away.'

'I can smash them with my hammer,' the blacksmith said, 'but I'm not a magician. I can't make them vanish.'

'No, but I can,' Brigit said with a grin. 'The Lysander collects us at ten o'clock tonight.'

'The town will be swarming with troops,' Legrande gasped. 'The Lysander may land but it will never take off again. After last night there will be patrols everywhere.'

'No. After last night every soldier in Bray will be surrounding the churchyard, waiting to round up every Resistance worker in town. Trust me, Monsieur Legrande, just be at the old airfield before ten with your lantern to light the landing path. It'll be fine.'

Brigit then went off to find Henri Caron and Marie Marcel and told them to meet, as usual, at Colette's barn. She knew one was a traitor and wasn't going to tell them of the landing until the last minute.

Then she headed back to the farm for lunch and a rest before night fell and the last great adventure began.

Berlin

'What time does the train arrive in Bray?' General Fischer asked.

'Ah, the line is still blocked after the sabotage,' Colonel Roth explained. 'We must go to Paris and then to Amiens. From there it's forty kilometres by car. We'll be there by dark, sir.'

'A tiring day.' The general sighed as he struggled to fasten the top button on the walrus neck that went with his walrus moustache.

'We could fly, but the British Air Force have been very active. They could shoot us down.'

'No, no, no, that would never do,' the general cried. 'Train and car it shall be. Just so long as I am in Bray to see the arrest of the whole Resistance group. A brilliant piece of work by Major Strauss... your uncle?'

'Yes, sir.'

'A genius. We need more men like him in the Gestapo... a man who is intelligent yet one who can strike like a viper when the time comes. I'm a bit like that you know?'

'You are, sir. Shall we go?'

'Lead the way, Roth. I shall remember this day for a long time.'

Chapter Forty-One

'They've been there for over a hundred years'

Bray-on-Somme

Night fell, and the full moon shone in a calm purple sky. Aimee and Brigit walked across the eastern fields of the farm to the airstrip. They each carried a small bag with the few clothes they had brought from Britain. They left behind the radio and the codebooks, the pencil bombs, the maps and the explosives. Colette would hide them and they'd be ready for another day.

To the west they could hear army trucks moving into place. If they hoped to trap secret agents while making that sort of noise they were wrong. A cat wearing ten bells had as much chance of catching a bird.

As it grew closer to ten o'clock the town finally fell silent. A light breeze from the west would carry the sound of the Lysander arriving long before anyone saw it. But the enemy would be too busy at the churchyard and the saboteurs would be ready.

Blacksmith Legrande stood by the gate to the field. 'Good evening, Charles,' Aimee said with a smile.

'Good evening, Madame Marcel,' Brigit said to the teacher. She had been unhappy when she'd arrived at the farm to be told of Aimee's escape that night.

'Good evening, Henri,' Aimee said to the reporter. 'Are we all ready?'

Two Resistance workers and one traitor muttered that they were.

'People in the town said someone was arrested by the Gestapo around half past eight last night,'

Marie Marcel said. 'It wasn't you, Madame Furst, was it?'

'It was,' Brigit said. 'And me too. But we talked our way out of it.'

'How?'

Brigit laughed. 'We just told them we were Gestapo agents pretending to be Resistance saboteurs.'

'And Major Strauss believed you?'

Brigit shrugged. 'He had to. You see, there really *is* a Gestapo spy in Bray. He knew that. He just didn't know who the man or woman was.'

'So how were you betrayed?'

'The traitor whispered our secret to old Corporal Rudolf in the dark.'

'Then we're all in danger,' Marie Marcel gasped. 'The traitor could name us all.'

Before she could answer, Brigit's ears picked up the faint humming like a distant bee. 'The Lysander. It's a few minutes early – the westerly wind must have blown it along,' she said. 'We'll have to hurry.' Aimee placed Blacksmith Legrande and Marie Marcel at the end of the runway where the plane would stop before it turned around and they climbed on board.

Brigit and Henri Caron ran to the far end of the airfield and peered into the sky. The Lysander made a black shape against the cream moon and they switched on their lanterns.

The plane waggled its wings to show it had seen them, then the engine's note dropped as the pilot cut his speed and began to circle towards the waiting group.

The plane landed. It was two minutes to ten. It turned, the glass hatch over the cockpit slid open and Aimee ran forward to pass the cases to the waiting pilot.

Marie Marcel stepped forward towards the tail of the plane. Blacksmith Legrande took a sock filled with sand from his coat pocket and hit her over the back of the head with it.

*

In Bray churchyard there was silence apart from the creaking of the leather Gestapo boots and the shuffle of army boots over the grassy mounds that had covered the coffins for hundreds of years.

'Are you certain the Resistance will turn up?' General Fischer asked.

'Oh yes, sir. We have the names of the traitors willing to join here. Camille Olivier, Hugo Philippe and Bastien Robert.'

'And the Gestapo spy in their midst? Will they be here too?'

'Yes, sir.'

'We'd better be careful to arrest them with the others, so no one suspects. We can use them again. What was the brave woman's name, Colonel Roth?'

'She's a teacher. Marie Marcel, sir,' Roth replied.

'That wasn't the name she gave me,' Major Strauss said. 'It was Furst. Aimee Furst. Marcel is just her code name.'

'These agents change their names to keep their secrets,' Roth grumbled. 'I just wish they'd tell me in Berlin when they do it.'

There was loud groaning and a clack of turning wheels as the clock on the church tower moved forward and the bell began to strike the hour. Ten times it sounded and the air trembled into silence.

A faint light appeared between the gravestones. 'Switch that torch off, Corporal Rudolf,' Major Strauss said. 'What are you doing?'

'Reading the gravestones, sir,' the old soldier said.

'We are waiting to capture Resistance workers while you read gravestones?'

'That's what I was about to tell you, sir,' the corporal said. 'They're already here.'

'What? Where?' General Fischer choked. 'Where?'

'Under the ground, sir. They've been there for over a hundred years. I thought those names sounded familiar,' Rudolf went on sadly. 'Every month I change the flowers on the graves of some of my comrades from the last war and those are the names on some of the other gravestones. See for yourself, sir,' he said, flashing a torch at the moss-covered headstones. 'Camille Olivier, Hugo Philippe and Bastien Robert.'

'That Furst woman lied to us,' Major Strauss groaned.

'Not really, sir. She said those three would be here at ten o'clock tonight… and they are.'

*

Blacksmith Legrande lifted the limp body of Marie Marcel into the Lysander where she lay twisted on the floor. Brigit climbed in after her and checked that the gag and ropes that bound the traitor would stay tight till they landed.

Aimee turned to little Henri Caron who was still dazed at what had happened. 'I trusted her,' he said. 'Why did she do it?'

'The SOE back in Britain will find out when they question her. Meanwhile you are safe.' The blacksmith walked over towards them. Aimee went on, 'You have both been heroes. For now, you need a rest from the dangers. One day, when the British and American armies are ready to land in France, Mr Churchill will send an SOE agent – it may be me, it may be someone else. They will need your help. They will need your sharp eyes, Henri. They will need your strong arms, Charles.'

'How will we know?' Henri asked.

'We will send a radio message to my mother, Colette, at the farm. Mr Churchill and our American friends will invade and drive the Germans back to where they came from. The Resistance in France must make our invasion easier by destroying the Germans from inside the country. You have been heroes; you shall be heroes again.'

Aimee shook hands with each of them then kissed them on their cheeks. They were cheeks that were wet and salty with tears. She climbed the short ladder into the cockpit and squeezed in beside Brigit. Her feet rested on the groaning shape of a traitor.

The two men ran to the end of the field to light the path for the plane. The roar of the engine split the air and moments later it was soaring over the quiet town of Bray.

A hundred German soldiers and four Gestapo officers looked up at it.

The oldest and fattest of the officers turned to the small and chubby one. 'So, Major Strauss, while we have been chasing phantom Resistance workers, the real ones are flying off to safety.'

The major's mouth was too dry with fear to answer. He nodded.

'Do you have a warm coat, Major Strauss?'

'Yes, sir,' the man croaked.

'You will need it. Pack your bag. You are off to Russia.'

Chapter Forty-Two

'We will accept nothing less than full victory'

June 1941–May 1945: Coventry, England

The Furst family settled in Coventry. The haters of Castle Bromwich were fifteen miles away. Marius was released from internment and changed his name to Foster to avoid the people of his new home town treating him like an enemy. If anyone asked him about his accent he told them he was Polish and had escaped just before the Germans invaded in 1939.

Life was quiet. Brigit went to a new school. She couldn't settle. Aimee began work in a factory. She found it dull. Brigit lied about her age and went to work alongside her maman. It made life better for them both.

At the start of 1944 the SOE asked Aimee to return to France. The fightback against the German invaders would begin soon. The date was secret. Aimee left to lead the old Resistance group in Bray. Her trusty helpers were a blacksmith and a newspaper reporter. But now there were a dozen more desperate to help.

This time Brigit had to stay behind. Every week Major Ellis visited Marius and Brigit with news. The Germans were being crushed by armies from the south and the east. The enemy hadn't enough men to spare to seek out and destroy the Resistance fighters. It was the Resistance doing the destroying.

At last the news was announced. The invasion from the west had begun. British and American troops crossed the English Channel and landed on the beaches of north-west France.

As Mr Churchill had said back in 1942, '*This is not the end, it is not even the beginning of the end, but it is perhaps the end of the beginning.*'

On 6 June 1944 the American leader General Eisenhower told his troops, '*You will bring about the destruction of the German war machine, the elimination of Nazi tyranny over the oppressed peoples of Europe, and security for ourselves in a free world. Your task will not be an easy one. Your enemy is well trained, well equipped, and battle-hardened. He will fight savagely. The free men of the world are marching together to victory. We will accept nothing less than full victory.*'

Brigit and Marius listened in silence to the BBC radio report. The general finished, '*Good luck, and let us all beseech the blessings of Almighty God upon this great and noble undertaking.*'

'We all pray that,' Marius said.

'You want to see the defeat of your own people?' Brigit asked.

'No. Only the evil ones. The Nazis,' he said. 'For the sake of all the good Germans.'

And their prayers were granted.

A year later the war drew to a close. France had been set free when Major Ellis delivered the message: 'Aimee is on her way home.'

Epilogue

Tuesday, 8 May 1945:
Coventry, England

The city streets hummed like the tram rails under the rolling steel wheels. But this time it was the tramping footsteps of the Coventry people marching towards the centre that made the rails ring.

The green glow of gas lamps lit the smiling faces and turned the bombed buildings into smiles with broken teeth.

'Will you be going to the victory party in the centre?' Brigit asked. Her father and mother looked at one another and shook their heads. 'No. The people don't want to see a German in the middle of their happiness.'

'You're French, Maman.'

Aimee shrugged. 'And the British believe they fought the war to save the French. They hate the Germans. They despise the French. But you go, Brigit. Start making good memories after the bombs, the Blitz and the bitterness. Tonight will be a fresh start.'

Brigit put on a light coat and stepped out of the front door into a river of excited people. Most of them spoke in low voices and added to the hum that swelled as they met with other streams from side streets and alleys.

Families kept their heads together, but odd single men and women walked with their heads up, looking at the darkening sky and breathing in the warm summer air of victory.

One lone girl looked across and caught Brigit's eye then looked away, frowning. She wore a worn and faded brown coat and had rubbed a red powder into her cheeks and lips to make them rosy. Her straw hat was shapeless, but a new red, white and blue ribbon made it cheerful as a sparrow.

The girl looked again, and her thin lips fell open in a small 'o' of surprise. 'Brigit?' she cried. 'Brigit Furst?'

Brigit nodded, uncertain. She knew she should have known the girl's face, but it was too thin and pinched. 'It's me,' the girl went on. 'You remember me? Gladys Turnbull? We was at school together – before the war.'

'Of course,' Brigit said faintly, remembering the girl who had spent years trying to bully her. 'How've you been?'

'It seems ages ago – six years. We was just kids, but we had a good time, didn't we?'

'I guess so.'

Gladys threw her arms round Brigit and it was like being hugged by a skeleton. 'I mean you was the clever one at the top of the class and I was at the bottom. But we got on, didn't we?' She stopped for a moment, but the flowing crowd forced them to keep walking towards the city centre. 'We wasn't evacuated together, was we? I was sent to a horrible place. Farm in Wales. What about you?'

'A small village in Wales. I didn't stay long,' Brigit said.

'Yeah you got out. Don't blame you. The rest of us wasn't far behind, you know. We made an escape plan. The milk lorry stopped at the farm gates every morning and one of the lads knew how to drive. Well, the driver got out to load the milk churns, we piled in and drove off. I think the language that driver used was terrible.'

'You think?'

'Well, he was shouting in Welsh so we never really knew. What a laugh. We ran out of petrol at a place called Bewdley and walked the rest of the way.'

'Well done, Gladys.' Brigit smiled.

'I bet you never made no great escape like that… and it was all my idea. They was good days.'

Suddenly she grabbed Brigit's arm and pulled on it in excitement. 'And we won! Are you going to the victory parade?' Brigit nodded. 'Of course, I should be *in* the parade,' Gladys burbled on. 'When I escaped from Wales I went to the Spitfire factory where my mum worked, told them I was fourteen and did cleaning. But after a couple of years they taught me how to work the machines and made the planes that beat the Jerries. I used to hate them Jerries. Hate them.'

'But you forgive them because we won?' Brigit asked.

'Nah, nothing like that. It's a funny thing but one day I was working on a lathe, the tool slipped and I gashed me hand. Quite nasty it was. They sent me to the medical room and I was nearly fainting with loss of blood.' She held up a skinny hand to show a deep purple scar that ran across the palm.

'They had this doctor there,' the girl went on. 'He was the kindest man you ever met. I had trouble understanding him – me being faint and him being foreign. And then he says he was sorry, but he was German. The only German I ever met in my life and he was normal as you and me.'

'Yes, most of them are,' Brigit said quietly.

Gladys slowed again and was pushed forward by the people behind. 'Oh, I forgot, your dad was a Jerry wasn't he? Did they lock him up – intern him – when the war was on? Have they let him out yet?'

'They let him out very soon after the war started, because he was a good doctor and the factories needed all the doctors they could get.'

This time Gladys did stop. 'He didn't work at the Spitfire factory, did he?'

'He did.'

'What? All those secrets? They trusted him? Why?'

'Because he's a good man, Gladys.'

Gladys frowned and thought about it as she moved slowly forward. 'So he must have been the one that stitched me up?'

'I think he must,' Brigit said.

The thin girl's face went tight. 'Tell him thanks from me, will you? There was me doing me bit for Britain and he was helping us as well, doing his bit.'

Brigit looked around her. 'People are people, wherever they come from, he says.'

Gladys nodded fiercely.

A party of children wore the paper Union Jack hats they'd all been given. They ran along the crowded road, giggling. Loud dance music played in the Railway Hotel and dancers spilled out into the street and tangled with the children who joined them in twirls and skips and sways.

The music stopped suddenly and people were shouting, 'Quiet, quiet. It's Mr Churchill.'

Everyone fell silent and looked up at the balcony of the hotel as if they expected the prime minister to appear. Instead some workmen in brown overalls set up two large speakers pointing into the street. After crackles and hisses, screeches and squeals, the speakers settled and the distant voice of Mr Churchill could be heard.

'*My dear friends, this is your hour... a victory of the great British nation as a whole. Did anyone want to give in?*'

The crowd shouted, 'No.'

'*Were we downhearted?*'

'No.'

'*The lights went out and the bombs came down. But every man, woman and child in the country had no thought of quitting the struggle.*'

Cheers.

'*I say that in the long years to come, the people of this island will look back to what we've done, and they will say "do not despair, do not give in to violence and tyranny, march straight forward and die if need be – unconquered".*'

Long cheers.

'*Now we have emerged from one deadly struggle – a terrible foe has been cast on the ground and awaits our judgment and our mercy.*'

'He means the Germans,' Gladys whispered.

Churchill went on to say the war with Japan was still going on. The Americans were fighting it but, '*We will go hand and hand with them. Even if it is a hard struggle we will not be the ones who will fail.*'

This time the cheering went on a long time and faded as the dancing crowds began to sing their favourite wartime songs:

Roll out the barrel, we'll have a barrel of fun.
Roll out the barrel, we've got the blues
on the run.

A group of children burst from a side street dragging a huge straw model with a mask of the German leader Adolf Hitler. 'We're gonna burn him on a bonfire like Guy Fawkes,' a tiny child screamed in delight.

A quieter group headed up towards the bombed-out cathedral for a service in the ruins. Some carried flowers to remember the loved ones they'd lost and some dabbed at their cheeks to scrub away the silent tears. In all the joy there was pain.

'So what did you do, Brigit? Did you do your bit?'

Brigit thought a while. 'You were building Spitfire planes... I was making bombs.'

Gladys smiled happily. 'Munitions. Making bombs to drop on Jerry's head.'

'Something like that,' Brigit muttered.

'You did your bit too then?'

'I think so.'

Gladys hugged the arm of her new friend hard and used her sharp elbows to get to the front of the barrier that kept the crowds away from the road.

Someone started singing the sentimental–

'I'll say a prayer while I am gone;
I'll pray each night, and pray each morn;
Though we're apart, we're not alone,
We'll live to share a peaceful dawn.'

Gladys gave a bitter laugh. 'I sang that with little Jessie Burdess when we went home after we escaped from Wales. Remember Jessie?'

'I remember her well.'

'But we never did meet again. There was the night they bombed the cathedral. Jessie's factory got it. They never found her.' Gladys flared with anger. 'What did Jessie do to deserve that, eh? She never hurt no one. It isn't fair.'

Brigit said nothing but gave a silent prayer for the girl she remembered.

There was the distant sound of a brass band leading the parade and the crowd began to raise their voices – some singing songs from the war, some cheering and others weeping silently.

'Why aren't you in the parade?' Brigit asked. 'The workers from the Spitfire factory have a banner. You deserve to be there, marching behind it.'

Glady's face turned pink despite the green glow of the gas street lamps. 'I'd show them up. Look at me. Shabby as a scarecrow. Our house was bombed when I was at work – lost me Sunday best clothes. No, I don't want no medals or parades. If they give everyone a medal then the medals won't be worth anything, will they? They're just for special people. You know what I mean?'

'I know. They tried to give my mother a medal. She refused. She said the same as you, Gladys.

305

She was just doing what she could to help us beat the enemy.'

Gladys nodded like a wise old woman. 'It was enough to know she did her bit. Like you, Brigit, with your bombs. Like me with my Spitfires.'

The music began to swell, and the cheers almost drowned the victory trumpets and trombones as the band stomped through the main street. The girl raised her hat and waved it – the only red, white and blue she had. She looked happily into the eyes of Brigit Furst. 'We won. And not just that. It was thanks to the likes of us. We did our bit.'